What the critics are saying

"Rick and Jennifer find a mutual attraction and the hot bedroom scenes that follow almost set the pages on fire. A must read for those romantic souls who also want it to be erotic. I know I will be looking forward to reading more of her work in the future." – *Judith Saul for Sensual Romance*

"For anyone looking for a sweet endearing story that will stick with you, this is it." - *April Taylor for Sensual Romance*

Ellora's Cave Publishing, Inc.

PO Box 787

Hudson, OH 44236-0787

ISBN # 1-84360-449-3

Edited by Cris Brashear.

Cover art by Darrell King.

Warning: The following material contains strong sexual content meant for mature readers. *Full Bodied Charmer* has been rated NC-17, erotic, by a minimum of three independent reviewers. We strongly suggest storing this book in a place where young readers not meant to view it are unlikely to happen upon it. That said, enjoy…

FULL BODIED CHARMER

Written by

Marilyn Lee

With special thanks to Jen Marie from NYC, who graciously suggested several titles for this story, including the one I finally settled on.

Chapter One

Rick Markham walked down the short corridor from his office and looked around the half-opened door into the office at the other end of the passage. His partner and best friend, Troy Hunter, sat in his chair, smiling at a picture on his desk, oblivious to everything around him.

Rick grinned. As usual, at the end of a long day he found Troy staring at the picture of Angie and their daughter Sherri. Daydreaming about them again. He shook his head. Even after nearly three years of marriage, Troy still seemed as much in love with Angie as when he'd first married her.

Angie was sweet and Rick had encouraged Troy to admit his feelings for her. He'd still been a little surprised when Troy married her less than a year after meeting on a cruise to nowhere, almost four years earlier.

When he'd talked Troy into going on that cruise, he'd never suspected Troy would meet and fall for a woman so different from the ideal they both had of a tall, slender, beautiful blonde. Angie, although sweet, was a rather shy, full-figured brunette. Nevertheless, she had managed to knock Troy off his feet within a few days.

"Ready to call it a day?" he asked.

Clearly startled, Troy looked up. "Ah, yeah. What about you? Ready for your big night tomorrow?"

Rick frowned and slipped into the seat in front of Troy's desk. "I still can't believe I let you talk me into agreeing to participate in that silly bachelor auction."

Troy grinned. "Come on, Rick. This is a high profile charity event. It'll be good PR for Hunter & Markham to participate, in addition to helping needy kids. Since Hunter's very happily married that leaves Markham as the lucky guy who'll get to have a bunch of single women with money bid for the chance to spend an evening with him."

"Sounds like a ball," he said dryly.

"Oh, come on. You just might enjoy yourself."

"How likely is that?"

Troy shrugged. "It can happen. When I let you talk me into going on that cruise to nowhere, I never thought I'd meet the woman I intend to spend the rest of my life with. At the very least, you should keep an open mind."

"Well…maybe," he agreed grudgingly.

"That's the spirit." Troy got to his feet and slipped on his jacket. "Well, I'm heading home."

Rick glanced at his watch. Five thirty-five. "So you want to hit Pauly's for a beer on the way?"

Troy shook his head and crossed the floor. "A beer?"

Rick arched a brow. Troy had given up drinking when he'd been stopped for suspicion of driving under the influence several years earlier. "Okay, a beer for me and a seltzer water for you."

"Can't." He flicked out his office light and nodded toward the door.

Rick preceded him out the door and into the hallway. "Why not?" But he knew. Ever since Sherri's birth, Troy spent every single available moment at home. Angie had confided to him that Troy would spend hours just sitting beside Sherri's crib, touching, kissing, and staring at her with a look of wonder on his face and love in his eyes.

Of course, Rick could understand that since he was inclined to stare at Troy and Angie with more than a trace of envy when they were together. They were so obviously in love, and in lust, with each other.

"So what? You planning to spend the night staring at Sherri again?"

Troy grinned. "Man, she's amazing, isn't she?"

He nodded. "She sure is. Watching the three of you together has...I've been thinking lately that it's time I found a wife and had a kid or two of my own."

Troy nodded. "Have you told your mom?"

"And risk having her try to push me at every single woman she can find under sixty?"

Troy laughed. "Stop exaggerating. Your mom is much too subtle for that."

"Maybe. Nevertheless, I'll tell her *after* I find the woman I want to marry."

"Got any likely prospects in mind?"

"No."

Troy got a faraway look in his eyes. "Marry the right woman and you'll never regret it or miss being single."

Troy had certainly married the right woman, Rick thought as he drove home, skipping Pauly's. After changing into sweats, he broiled a steak, baked a couple potatoes, tossed a salad, and ate in front of the large screen television in his den. Although the meal was good, he couldn't help comparing his solitary dinner with the one Troy and Angie would be sharing.

He shook his head. Yep. It was definitely time to start looking for a woman he could settle down with. Nevertheless, his immediate need was for sex. He'd look through his phone book and find someone to spend a few hours in bed with. He half rose, then abruptly sank back into his chair. If he were going to get serious about finding a woman he could fall in love with and marry, he supposed he'd better stop his late night booty calls.

He'd spent the last six months in a series of one-night stands with a few women who meant very little to him and were little more than warm bodies. Although they were all beautiful and great in bed, he hadn't found any of them satisfying on any level beyond the purely physical. He couldn't imagine any of them wanting to lose their figures during pregnancy.

He sighed. He supposed he was going to have to start from scratch. He could do that, but he'd better find a woman soon or his balls would be completely blue.

* * * * *

"You're not dressed."

Jennifer Rose turned from the open closet doors. Her best friend, Cherica Martin stood in her bedroom door.

As usual, Cherica was dressed to 'conquer.' She wore a long, sleek, dark silk dress that clung to all her considerable curves and took a daring plunge just above her breasts. Her dark blonde hair was swept up into an elegant chignon. Her pretty face was flawlessly made up. The dark mauve dress and her beautiful eyes provided the perfect contrast to her beautiful golden skin. Cherica was fond of saying that, as the child of an interracial couple, she had the best of both worlds. Looking at the stunning picture she made, Jennifer whole-heartedly agreed.

"I hope you're not having second thoughts about tonight, Jenn."

Jennifer grimaced and turned to consider her slip- and stocking-clad body. She had long ago learned to accept the fact that she was always going to be full-figured. Just lately, she had been thrilled to discover there was a whole group of men who so preferred women her size that they were willing to pay several hundred dollars for the opportunity to spend a few hours alone with them. Julie, a mutual friend of hers and Cherica's, commanded such high fees as a full-figured escort that she'd quit her job as a computer technician and become a full-time escort.

It was thrilling and liberating to realize that the slender, supermodel types didn't have to have all the fun. Still, Jennifer spent an inordinate amount of time agonizing over which outfits and style of clothing best complimented her. She found choosing an appropriate outfit for their evening that night especially difficult.

She was having second thoughts, but decided to go through with their plans anyway. Tonight would be the first step in her plan to come out of her shell and enjoy herself more. Besides, as a full-time author, she eagerly welcomed each new experience as potential material for a new series of articles or a possible foundation on which to build a new book. "It's not that...exactly," she said, sighing. "I just can't decide what to wear."

"Oh. That's easy." Cherica crossed the room and removed a pink two-piece silk dress from the closet. "Wear this. You look really good in pink."

Jennifer wrinkled her brows in indecision. The dress in question had a low clinging bodice that provided a rather daring glimpse of her full breasts. The skirt portion fell into graceful folds just below her knees. "I don't know. This shows an awful lot of breast."

"In case you haven't noticed, most men are into breasts, especially big ones. So, what am I missing?"

She grinned. "You have a point there, but I think I'll go with this one." She reached into the closet and drew out a blue silk dress with a more modest neckline that still showcased her long legs.

Cherica grinned. "Okay, that'll work too. Now that we have your wardrobe settled, how about getting a move on?"

"How's Jayson?" Jennifer asked as she began dressing.

"Jayson?"

Jennifer paused and turned to look at Cherica, who sat on the side of her bed. "Yes, Jayson. You know...tall, lean...beautiful eyes...great kisser."

"Oh. That Jayson."

"Do we know more than one Jayson?"

"No," she admitted reluctantly.

"Then that's the one I'm talking about," she teased.

Cherica frowned suddenly. "A great kisser? You...you've kissed him?"

"No."

Cherica shrugged. "Then what do you mean great kisser?"

"I'm going by what you told me," she pointed out, arching a brow. "On several occasions, I might add."

Cherica blushed and looked away. "Oh."

"So how is he?"

"Oh. Well...he's...he's, you know...Jayson."

Jennifer turned and resumed her dressing to hide a smile. It always amazed her that while Cherica was so confident in herself as a full-figured woman, she was afraid to admit that she felt more than friendship for the man they'd both known since high school. Of course, there was a reason she was so reticent about her feelings. "How's Dave?"

"Dave?" Cherica sounded weary. "He's fine."

Maybe he was, but Cherica and Jayson weren't. Somehow, without saying a word, Cherica's over-protective brother Dave always managed to convey the impression that he would disapprove of a relationship between Cherica and Jayson Calihan. "Good. And everyone else?"

"Everyone's fine." Now that they were no longer talking about Jayson or Dave, Cherica's voice sounded more normal.

"Good." She zipped up her dress and turned to look at Cherica. "So. Will I do?"

Cherica grinned. "You'll more than do. You're absolutely gorgeous."

Jennifer cast a quick look at her reflection. Admittedly, the dress was flattering, and hopefully she wasn't quite the plain Jane, but saying she was gorgeous was stretching the truth a mite. She slipped on a pair of heels, donned the diamond stud earrings her mother had given her for her last birthday, and applied her favorite scent. She took a deep breath. "Okay. I'm as ready as I'm going to get."

Cherica smiled. "Oh, come on, we'll both have a ball tonight."

"Both? You mean you're actually going to bid on a man?"

Cherica arched a brow. "Of course I am. What's with the goofy question?"

"It's not all that goofy."

"Yeah, it's way goofy."

"Well, what's Jayson going to say?"

She watched as Cherica's beautiful face turned a warm shade of red. "Jenn, for the last time, there's nothing between me and Jayson. Nothing. Okay? We're friends. That's all."

"Would there be something more between you two if Jayson wasn't black?"

Cherica's eyes widened. "Jenn! Are you implying I'm prejudiced?! In case you're forgetting, my dad is black, remember?"

"Of course I remember, and I'm not implying you're prejudiced. How could you even suggest that?"

"Then what are you implying?"

She hesitated. It didn't seem the time to mention Dave's name. Besides, Cherica would only get defensive and their evening would be ruined. "Nothing much. Just that I think you and Jayson make a great couple."

"There's only one thing wrong with the picture you're painting, Jenn. We're not a couple."

No. Thanks to Dave. She shrugged. "I know. Subject closed. Okay?"

Cherica nodded. "Okay."

"All right. So. Let's go buy us a date."

"Not that we have to, but now you're talking. Let's go. The club will probably get crowded very quickly and I want to get a good seat."

An hour and a half later, they were seated near the front of the stage.

"Oh, Jenn, is he a hunk, or what?" Cherica whispered the question.

"Oh, yeah, baby," she whispered back.

"Want to bid on him?"

The man standing on the walkway was indeed striking. He was tall and handsome with the most beautiful blue eyes Jennifer had ever seen. He was nicely built, and he had a nice smile and gorgeous, shoulder-length blond hair. His fatal flaw, as far as she was concerned, was his near beauty. A man that attractive would not appreciate having to spend an evening with anything less than a perfect woman. Besides, she wasn't really into blonds anymore. These days she liked her men with dark hair, dark eyes, and big cocks nestled among dark pubic hair.

"He's a little too good-looking for me," she said. However, he would be perfect as the hero in her next erotic romance thriller.

"Sure you don't mean too blond?" Cherica challenged.

She nodded. "Okay. He's that, too. I think I'll save my money for a man not quite so…perfect."

"Or blond," Cherica added.

"Or blond," she admitted, shrugging.

Although Cherica was a natural blonde, they both agreed that blond men were generally too stuck on themselves to make good boyfriends. She thought of Mike; a tall, handsome blond she'd dated briefly in her freshman year of college. He'd been a great lover, and she'd been more than a little in love with him. The revelation that he'd taken her virginity on a dare had devastated her.

Two years later, in her junior year, she'd fallen for another blond, Danny, who'd dated her just so he could say he'd fucked a fat chick.

In her senior year, she had a brief affair with yet another blond, Hal. When she walked in on Hal with another woman, he'd calmly told her that his goal was to fuck every willing female on campus and that she couldn't really expect a man to get serious with a woman he couldn't pick up.

After that, she'd decided that the only thing certain about blond men was that they didn't know the meaning of the word fidelity.

"Yeah, maybe you're right," Cherica said and they exchanged smiles.

The blond wonder was quickly auctioned off. The next man, dark and good-looking, but rather short, also went quickly.

Two men later, an ebony hunk with warm dark eyes and a buff body that his well-cut suit emphasized, walked onto the stage. Cherica sucked in a breath, sat up, and quickly became embroiled in a bidding war with a tall, slender, blue-eyed blonde at a table to their left.

Jennifer nearly held her breath as Cherica called out four hundred dollars.

All eyes turned to the blonde, who sighed and sank back into her seat in defeat.

"And the lucky lady at table five has won an evening with bachelor number six. Ma'am, please proceed to the pledge table to make the final arrangements."

With her eyes shining and her cheeks flushed, Cherica rose to her feet. "Now your turn, Jenn."

They exchanged a wink before Cherica left their table.

Ten minutes later, a tall, attractive man with short, thick blond hair and blue-green eyes walked out onto the stage. Jennifer was about to dismiss him as just another pretty blond boy when he smiled. He had an amazing, Bruce Willis-type smile.

"Ladies, the bidding for this eligible bachelor will start at one hundred dollars. One hundred dollars," the Mistress of Ceremonies called out. "Do I have one hundred dollars?"

Jennifer responded without conscious thought. "One hundred dollars."

The man turned to look at her and she sucked in a breath. What beautiful eyes he had to go with that beguiling smile.

"I have one hundred dollars. One hundred dollars. Come on, ladies—"

"One hundred fifty," the blonde spoke.

The man's gaze shifted to the blonde and lingered there.

"I have one hundred fifty dollars. Do I have—"?

"Two hundred dollars," Jennifer called out.

"Two hundred dollars. I have two hundred dollars. Do I have—"?

"Two-fifty," the blonde interrupted.

"Two-fifty. Ladies, I have two hundred and fifty dollars. Do I have—"?

"Three hundred," Jennifer said, casting a wary look at the blonde.

"Three-fifty," the blonde countered, her eyes narrowing.

She was already way past the limit of two hundred and fifty dollars she had set for herself. But damned if she was going to lose a chance to spend an evening with a man with a Bruce Willis smile without a fight. "Four hundred," she said, and silently prayed the blonde would crumble as she had when Cherica had hit the four hundred dollar mark.

"Four-fifty," the blonde said, lifting her chin slightly.

"Four hundred fifty dollars. Ladies, I have four hundred fifty dollars. Do I have—"?

"Five hundred." Jennifer said and immediately wanted to kick herself. Five hundred dollars to spend a platonic night with a man she'd never see again? A man who clearly wanted the blonde to win the bidding war? God, she'd lost her mind. For that kind of money, she at least wanted a night of unbridled passion with a lusty, well-hung stud with big, hot hands and a raging hard-on.

The man reluctantly tore his gaze away from the blonde to look in her direction and Jennifer thought she saw a look of resignation and regret on his face.

"Five hundred dollars. Ladies, I have five hundred dollars. Do I have five hundred and fifty dollars?" The Mistress of Ceremonies looked at the blonde, who, after a long moment, gave a small, negative shake of her head. "And the lucky lady at table five has won an evening with bachelor number nine. Ma'am, please proceed to the pledge table to make the final arrangements."

"Way to go, Jenn, but what happened? In case you didn't notice, he has a head full of honey-blond hair."

She turned to find Cherica in her seat. She blinked at her in surprise. "Rica. I didn't hear you come back."

"No. You were too busy staring at tall, blond, and handsome," Cherica grinned at her. "Looks like we both lucked out."

"I can't believe I spent five hundred dollars on him," she said in disgust.

"Why not?"

"Why not? Did you see the way he was looking at the blonde? He wanted her to win."

Cherica shrugged. "Well, she didn't. Even though he's a blond, he looks like he's worth every penny."

"Damn." She was still feeling like kicking herself as she rose and made her way over to the pledge table at the back of the room.

She was nearly there before she realized that the man she'd bought a "date" with was also there. She forced herself to keep walking. She couldn't tell what he thought of her as he stood watching her approach, although he allowed his blue-green eyes to sweep briefly over her. She noticed with resignation that his gaze didn't linger.

The woman behind the table looked up and smiled at her. "You're the lucky lady who's scheduled an evening with bachelor number nine?"

Jennifer nodded, a smile tugging at her lips. Now there was a quaint way of saying she'd bought herself a date with a man who clearly wished she hadn't. "Yes."

"And your first name?"

"Jennifer."

"Jennifer, this is…" The woman glanced briefly at a form on the table in front of her. "Rick. Rick, this is Jennifer, your date for what I'm sure will be a lovely evening."

Boy, wasn't she the gracious one, Jennifer thought and turned to look at the man she'd spent five hundred dollars on. Man, but she felt awkward.

A brief smile touched his lips. "Hi."

She extended her hand and had it briefly engulfed in a warm clasp. "Hello."

He released her hand. "So we'll be spending an evening together?"

She nodded. *You'd better believe it, buster, and I intend to get my money's worth out of you.* "Ah…yes."

He inclined his head towards the pledge table. "I've given my phone numbers so I'll expect a call from you soon."

She nodded, suppressing a sigh. *Okay, Jennifer. Granted he's a big, good-looking guy; but remember, you've sworn off blonds, so don't go getting any crazy ideas.* She watched him walk away before she turned back to the table to give her name and credit card information. Despite her admonition to herself, she was already looking forward to spending an evening with him. And who knew? Maybe she'd luck out and get him to take her to bed for a night of passion before they said their goodbyes.

Chapter Two

"So what do you think Jayson will say?"

The question was followed by long a silence. Sighing, Jennifer looked up from the sketch she was making to find Cherica frowning at her. She and Cherica were sitting in her living room discussing the two hunks they'd bought dates with. They'd been laughing and feeling rather carefree and daring. Now, she saw that weary look she hated settled over Cherica's pretty face."What will he say about what?" she asked. "It's no concern of his what I do with my money or who I go out with."

When would she learn that just because she thought Cherica and Jayson were perfect for each other, that she couldn't push them together? She sighed and shook her head. "Rica, I'm a knucklehead. I'm sorry."

Cherica shrugged. "Jenn, I don't know how many ways I can tell you there's nothing between me and Jayson. We're friends and that's all we're ever going to be."

If that were true, it would be a crying shame. "Don't mind me. I'm just jealous because I don't have a kissing male friend like Jayson."

That brought a hint of color to Cherica's face. "Jayson and I...okay...I admit that we occasionally...kiss each other, but they're just friendly...pecks."

If Jenn had been sipping her herb tea, she would probably have choked. She'd seen some of the "friendly pecks" the two of them had exchanged over the years. Some of the kisses went on forever and were so intense, Jennifer got hot just watching them. At Christmas, Cherica and Jayson never let a single sprig of mistletoe go unutilized.

Schooling her face into what she hoped was a bland mask; she nodded and began sketching again, her hand flying over the sketchpad. Although she wasn't a professional artist or graphic designer, she liked to make the preliminary sketches for her cover art, to increase her chances of getting the cover she wanted for her books. Satisfied with her efforts, she turned the page and began a new sketch, this one from memory. "I know. I just meant what do you think he'll say as a friend?"

Cherica shrugged and took a long sip of her tea. "Who says I plan to tell him?"

"You're not going to tell him?"

"No." She sounded defensive. "Why should I?"

She continued sketching. "No reason, I guess."

"That's right and it's not as if anything's going to happen with this guy. We'll go out for our obligatory date, say goodbye at the end of the evening and never see each other again. What's to tell? Isn't that what you expect to happen with Blondie?"

Jennifer tossed her hair off her shoulders, glanced at her sketch, decided it was passable, and lay it face down on the sofa next to her. "He is rather blond, isn't he? Still, he has a Bruce Willis smile and a warm, deep voice." She grinned. "And he has a nice set of buns too."

Cherica arched a brow. "Nice buns?"

"Yeah, baby," she drawled and they collapsed into a fit of giggles, much as they'd done when they were teenagers. She sobered first. "If I'm lucky, I'll get a chance to pinch them."

Cherica ran a hand through her hair. "Just a pinch, huh?"

"Well...I wouldn't say no to a quick roll in the hay," she admitted.

Cherica's eyes widened. "You're going to sleep with another blond?"

She felt her cheeks heating up. "I know I said I'd never go anywhere near another blond, but I spent five hundred dollars on him and if I get the chance, I'm going to get something for my money besides conversation."

"Oooh. I heard that."

She shrugged. "Besides, it's been awhile since Jeff and I broke up and…well, to be frank, I'm feeling a little on the horny side."

Cherica nodded. "Hey, believe me, I can identify. A woman has needs just like a man."

And what she needed was to feel a man inside her. She shrugged. "I doubt if I'll get the chance. Did you see how he looked at the blonde who was bidding on him? I think he's one of those guys who likes his women blonde, slender and gorgeous; which leaves me out of the running on all three counts," she said. She grinned suddenly. "But if I should happen to get the chance, I'll show him what a full-figured woman is capable of in bed."

Cherica nodded. "Now you're talking. I just might do the same thing." She paused, frowning. "And if you dare to ask me what Jayson will say, I warn you, I'll cold stare you right back into last week."

Jennifer shuddered. Nothing had gone right the week before. Her car had broken down on the expressway; her editor had sent her latest novel about a modern day Frankenstein meets Cinderella back for major rewrites; and her widowed mother had called to tell her she'd started dating a younger man. "I wouldn't wish last week on my worst enemy. My lips are sealed. No more Jayson questions…at least for tonight."

Cherica cast her eyes ceiling ward. "You are impossible." She pointed to the sketch. "So? Who is it? Your blond Bruce Willis?"

"Guess again."

"Who? It's too late for twenty questions."

She grinned and held up the sketch, keeping her gaze on Cherica's face as she recognized the dark, lean lines of Jayson Calihan's handsome face. "What do you think?"

"It's...Jayson..."

"Yeah. I know. What do you think? Does it do him justice?"

"It's...well...it's...it's him." Cherica paused, biting her lip. "Ah...what are you going to do with it?"

"Nothing special. Would you...like it?"

"Me? Oh, well...I..." she sighed and shrugged. "Yes," she said quietly. "I would."

She carefully tore the page from the pad and handed it to Cherica when she approached.

Cherica went back to her seat and sat looking down at the sketch. "It's a nice likeness of him. Maybe I'll frame it and give it to his mom as a present...if you don't mind."

"Of course I don't." She bit her lip to hide a grin. She'd bet her next royalty check that Jayson's mother would never have more than a passing look at the sketch.

"Good."

She nodded and sipped at her tea, her thoughts turning towards Rick. What was his last name? Where did he live? What did he like in a woman? Would he at least kiss her goodnight after their date? His bottom lip had looked rather full. He was probably a great kisser. She refused to let her thoughts linger on the possibility of his being as well endowed as her previous blond lovers.

"Hey, anybody home?"

She blinked rapidly and looked at Cherica. "Sorry. Daydreaming."

"About Blondie?"

She shrugged. "Maybe."

Cherica arched a brow. "Maybe?"

She smiled. "Okay. I was thinking of him."

Cherica leveled a finger at her. "I think you need to come out of denial and admit that you prefer blond men."

"I don't!"

"Ah huh. If you say so."

"Rica!"

"Okay. Okay, you don't like blonds. You just spent five hundred dollars on him because you had an extra five bills lying around." She nodded. "Understand perfectly. I do the same thing myself every time I have five hundred dollars and nothing to do with it."

Jennifer's lips twitched and then she smiled. "Okay. You've made your point."

"So where are you taking him?

"Some place romantic where we can eat and dance. Any suggestions?"

"How about that waterfront restaurant on the South Street Pier? The lights are low, the music soft, and the booths high backed so you feel like you're alone, even when the place is packed."

"It's not very subtle," she said doubtfully.

"You want subtle or you want to get laid?"

"Oh, I definitely want to get laid."

"By Blondie?"

"Yes," she admitted. She sighed and shook her head. "Okay...I'm hopeless. I still like blonds, okay? Satisfied?"

Cherica grinned, tossing her head so that her blonde hair was sent cascading around her shoulders. "Who can blame you?" she asked, grinning. "Blondes are passionate lovers."

She laughed. "The ones I've known were certainly well-endowed."

"Hmm."

"Okay, now that we've settled that, where are you going to take Maurice?"

"To that new hotel near the airport. I hear they have a couple of four star restaurants and wonderful waterbeds."

Cherica arched a brow. "I'll let you know if the rumors about the waterbeds are true."

Although she grinned like a co-conspirator, she couldn't help feeling that Jayson was going to be crushed if he ever found out.

They discussed what they would wear on their respective dates and finished their tea before Cherica walked down the hall to catch the elevator to her apartment, four floors below.

Jennifer undressed and got into bed. Her last thoughts before she succumbed to sleep were of Rick. She smiled, deciding she was going to wear the two-piece silk for their date to increase her chances of scoring for the night.

* * * * *

Driving home from the bachelor auction, Rick tried not to feel disgruntled. Okay, so the blonde supermodel type he'd been hoping would make the winning bid on him had folded. The evening hadn't been a total loss. He'd done his bit for charity and he was only required to spend a few hours with the woman who had "won" a date with him. While she was definitely not his type, he didn't think he'd have any problem spending a few hours in her company.

Winning bidders had a two-week period in which to set a date. Hopefully, she'd call him within the coming week. If she did, they could set up an immediate date. If his luck held, he could be finished with his obligation to her by the weekend. Then he would use the number the slender blonde, Carolyn, had passed to another woman to hand to him as he was leaving the club.

Although he itched to call Carolyn and make a date with her, it didn't seem sporting to see her before he fulfilled his obligation to the woman who'd spent five hundred dollars just to spend a few hours with him.

Five hundred dollars was a lot of money to spend for a few hours with a man she'd never see again. The least he could do was play fair and make sure she got her money's worth—up to a point, at least. While they were together, he would give her his undivided attention.

At home, he undressed, got in bed, and fell asleep almost immediately. He woke in the middle of the night and lay staring up at his darkened ceiling in dismay. His cock was semi hard and he was aroused. Now why the hell should a dream of the woman he'd met briefly that night stir him sexually? He was not Troy. He was not into full-figured women. He frowned. Although he had to admit that the woman he'd be spending an evening with had had a certain...something.

He wasn't sure if that "something" was her beautiful, almost olive skin tone; her long, dark, thick hair; or her rather stunning silver-gray eyes that had shimmered with a hint of passion when he'd briefly looked into them. Then there was that smile of hers...slow, warm, intimate, and just a little on the bewitching side. What was her name? Jennifer?

He'd bet more than one man had forgotten her size after losing himself in the depths of her enchanting gaze. He frowned and shook his head. *Okay, Rick, so she has a beautiful smile and a bottomless gaze. So what? Don't lose it. Get through your date with her and move on. Period.*

It was annoying that he lay awake thinking about her before he finally fell asleep again. He felt better when he woke in the morning from a scorching dream of the beautiful Carolyn, with whom he fully intended to pursue a relationship. That was more like it, he thought as he took a cold shower to banish his horny thoughts of her. First he'd do his duty date, then he'd have his pleasure date. Hopefully with lots of sex.

As he got out of the shower, his phone rang. He wrapped a towel around his waist and went back to his bedroom to answer it. "Hello?"

"Good morning, Rick."

He smiled. "Angie. Sweets, how are you?"

"Good. Listen, I'm about to make buttermilk pancakes and sausage with eggs. If you're not busy or otherwise engaged, we'd love to have you join us."

"Otherwise engaged on a Sunday morning?"

"You know…with a woman."

He hadn't been regularly 'otherwise engaged' on a Sunday morning for nearly a year when he and Debbi, a pretty blonde stewardess, had broken up when she'd been transferred to a transatlantic run. "And if I'm otherwise engaged?" he asked, amused that she sounded shy.

"Bring her too, if she'd like to come."

"Thanks. I'll be there in half an hour."

"Good. With or without?"

"Without. See you soon, sweets."

He finished dressing, after which he left home. Angie met him at the door with Sherri on her hip. He kissed her on both cheeks and lifted Sherri out of her arms. Sherri, her dark eyes shining, her chubby cheeks flushed, wrapped both small arms around his neck and planted a wet kiss on his cheek.

He hugged her close and brushed his nose against her neck. "How's my favorite, pretty little darling?" he asked.

"Unca Icky." Sherri giggled and rewarded him with another wet kiss. He responded by kissing both her cheeks repeatedly.

"Okay you two, break up the love fest," Troy said, lifting Sherri from his arms.

Rick watched as Sherri immediately pressed a wet kiss against Troy's mouth. "Daddy."

Angie slipped her arm through Rick's and urged him into the foyer. "How are you?" she asked as they walked down the hall, arm-in-arm.

He cast a quick, envious look over his shoulder at Troy. "Not as well as Troy," he said dryly. He smiled down at her. "He's spitting lucky to have you and Sherri."

"We're lucky to have him too," she countered, her eyes softening as they always did when she talked about Troy.

Would a woman ever sound so pleased to be his wife and woman? Damn, Troy was one lucky guy.

The four of them had breakfast in the kitchen. While they ate, Sherri moved around the circular table, demanding bits of food from each adult. After licking all the syrup off Troy's pancakes, she got off of Troy's lap and looked at Angie.

"No way," Angie told her, shaking her head firmly. "Today I'm eating my pancakes with the syrup on them for a change."

Sherri immediately climbed onto Rick's lap and smiled up at him. "I ick Unca Icky's 'cakes?" she asked.

"Sure you can, darling," he said, running his fingers through her dark hair.

Angie shook her head. "Rick, you're as bad as Troy. You're putty in her hands," she said in an amused voice.

"How can I deny her anything when she smiles, calls me Unca Icky, and looks up at with me with those big, gorgeous eyes of hers?" he asked, grinning.

"Between the two of you, she's going to be spoiled rotten," she complained, still smiling.

Sherri finished licking his pancakes, rewarded him with a sticky kiss, and climbed back into Troy's lap.

After breakfast, Angie went to bathe Sherri, and Rick and Troy settled into the den to watch the sports channel.

"So how did last night go?"

He shrugged. "Okay."

"Just okay? What's the matter?" Troy grinned. "Didn't you get bought?"

"As a matter of fact, I did get bought," he said.

"Yeah? For how much?"

"Can you say five hundred?" he queried.

Troy's eyes widened. "As in dollars?"

"Yes." He grinned. "There was a bidding war between two women. Two *young* women."

"How young?"

He shrugged. "They both looked to be in their twenties."

"And two twenty-something women wanted to spend a couple of hundred dollars on a man your age?"

"Hey, I'm younger than you, buddy," he reminded him.

Troy grinned. "Big deal. So that would make you...what? Forty-two?"

"Forty," he said. "And apparently they both like older men."

"No sh—ah, stuff. I meant stuff." He glanced around, saw that neither Sherri nor Angie were in the room and sighed in relief.

Rick concealed a smile with difficulty. Since Sherri's birth, Troy had made a conscious effort to give up profanity. "No...ah, stuff."

"So. What's she like?"

"How do I know what she's like? I saw her for a few minutes."

"What does she look like?"

He hesitated. "Ah...she's...ah...like Angie."

"Like Angie? How?"

"She's dark and full-figured."

"Ah. Bummer," Troy said.

"Why?"

The question seemed to surprise Troy. "Why? Because we both know what you think of full-figured women."

He remembered some of the unkind remarks he'd made about full-figured women in general and Angie in particular and squirmed in his seat. He'd been a first class idiot. "I've said some things about women that I shouldn't have and no longer believe," he said hastily.

"So you're saying what? That you don't mind that you have to spend an evening with a large woman?"

"Not overly, no. She's...ah...she has a great smile and an amazing pair of silver-gray eyes. I can take her for an evening. No problem."

"Oh. Good."

He nodded. What would Troy say if he admitted that he'd had an erotic dream of Jennifer? He probably wouldn't believe him. Hell, he barely believed it himself. But no matter. He would do his duty and forget her. "Actually, I expect to have a fairly decent time."

"Hmm."

"But after I've done my civic duty by her...there was this gorgeous blonde at the auction who passed me her number. And I am definitely going to call her."

Troy smiled, shaking his head. "Still looking for the perfect blonde bombshell huh?"

He shrugged. "What if I am? Is there any crime in liking blondes?"

"No." Troy held up his hands, palms out. "Hey, I used to like them myself...until I met and fell in love with Angie."

"Angie is a remarkable woman."

Troy smiled and his voice had softened when he spoke again. "Yes. And she's everything I need and want in a woman. I can't imagine how I was ever happy before I met her. Having her as my wife...she completes me." He grinned and shrugged. "I know that sounds corny, but—"

"You know, actually, it doesn't. I know it works for you and her. That's all that matters. And the two of you have produced the sweetest little girl I've ever seen."

Troy's grin widened. "Sherri is amazing, isn't she? She's perfect. I mean when I look at her and know that I had a part in her birth...it's an incredible feeling being her father and Angie's husband."

Rick nodded, feeling that hint of envy tighten in his gut. He was happy for Troy, but damned if he wasn't more than a little jealous also.

He noticed the speculative look on Troy's face and frowned. "What?"

"About this woman?"

"What about her?"

"You're not planning to hop in the sack with her a few times and then dump her, are you?"

"No! What makes you think I have any intention or interest in sleeping with her?"

"I know you, man. Your voice deepened and you got that 'I'm on the prowl for some pus—'" Troy paused and glanced around, apparently to make sure they were still alone before continuing. "'—for sex' look when you mentioned her."

He frowned at Troy. "She's not my type."

"Okay. She's not your type. Just don't dog her."

"I don't dog women, Troy. I've been honest about my intentions in every relationship I've been involved in, be it meaningful or of the one-night stand variety."

"Okay." Troy held up his hands. "It's none of my business and I'm butting out."

"That's not what I meant, Troy. I just don't like the idea of your assuming I plan to dog her."

"Let's face it, Rick, your track record with women has been a little on the...shady side...like my own before Angie. And before you say I'm busting your balls, I'm not."

He didn't much like the picture Troy painted of his character. His displeasure was fueled by the knowledge that Troy wasn't far off the mark. He shook his head. "Troy, you have no idea what my view of women is," he snapped.

"Okay. I said I was butting out, although I don't know why I should."

"What?"

"I mean you didn't butt out when I was being a butthead about Angie."

"That was different. You were being too stupid to admit that you were in love with her and that she was perfect for you."

"So naturally you felt bound to stick your nose in where it didn't belong."

"If I hadn't, you might have let Angie slip through your fingers."

Troy shook his head. "No way. I admit I was having a hard time admitting how I felt about her, but there was no way I wouldn't have eventually made my move."

"Yeah. Right."

They stared at each other in silence for several moments, before they both started laughing.

Rick spent the entire day with Troy and his family. After dinner, he kissed Angie and Sherri and headed home.

His phone was ringing as he entered his house. He lifted the cordless phone off the table in the front hall. "Hello?"

"Rick?"

He nodded. "Yes." He frowned. The voice wasn't familiar.

"This is Jennifer."

"Jennifer?"

"Yes. We met Saturday...well, I bought a date with you then," she said.

"Oh. Jennifer. Hi."

"Hi. I'm calling to schedule our date."

"Ah, yes," he said, surprised at how pleased he felt at hearing from her so soon. "When are we going out?"

"Well...are you free for dinner on Wednesday or Thursday?"

"I'm free both evenings. Which shall it be?"

"Wednesday then."

"Wednesday it is. What time?"

There was a noticeable pause before she replied. "Let's get an early start. How about five-thirty? Is that too early?"

"Five-thirty is fine. Where can I pick you up?"

"Pick me up? Oh. I thought…I was planning to pick you up. After all, I'm taking you out," she pointed out.

"So you are. How about we compromise and meet in the middle? Where are we going?"

"The River Rooms."

"Ah."

"Do you…know it?"

"Yes."

"I thought we could dance after dinner if you don't mind."

To his surprise, he didn't mind the thought of dancing with her in the least. "No. Why don't we meet at five-thirty at the parking lot on Fourth and Spring Garden? We can leave your car there and take mine the rest of the way."

"Okay. We have tentative reservations for six 'o'clock."

"Great. I'll see you then."

"Okay. See you then."

He was surprised to find that his cock had hardened while they talked. After he hung up, he undressed and headed for the shower. Once there, he soaped up his body and then slowly jerked himself off. He kept his eyes closed and pretended the hand on his cock was smaller and more feminine and attached to a woman with a pair of mesmerizing silver-gray eyes.

After he came, he finished his shower and climbed into bed, where he lay fantasizing first about Jennifer and then Carolyn. He drifted to sleep with a semi-hard cock. Damn, but he needed some pussy.

Chapter Three

When Rick pulled into the Fourth Street parking lot, he immediately noticed Jennifer sitting in her car. He parked a few spaces over and walked to her vehicle. She watched his approach. When he neared her car, she smiled at him.

He blinked and took a deep breath. Damn, but she had an incredible smile and absolutely beautiful eyes. And she knew how to dress, he thought as she got out of her car. She had on a pretty pink dress that provided an intriguing view of her ample cleavage. Her breasts were delightfully large.

There were few things sexier than a beautiful woman with big tits. What would it be like to touch and kiss those luscious looking mounds and tongue her nipples? His cock stirred and he found it difficult to tear his gaze away from her breasts and look into her eyes. Once he had, he could see she was aware of the effect the sight of her breasts was having on his libido.

Her smile was wondrous: shy, yet tinged with a hint of confidence he found incredibly alluring.

"Hi." She spoke first and widened her smile.

He felt his own lips turning up in a smile and he eagerly reached for her hand. "Hi, Jennifer. Nice to see you again."

"It's nice to see you again, too." Her voice and gaze were warm and welcoming.

He stared down into her eyes. Why would such a lovely, sexy woman have to buy a date? There must be any number of men waiting to take her to bed. He sure as hell did.

He released her hand and nodded towards his car. "Is it okay if we take my car?"

"What's the matter? Don't trust a woman driver?" She arched her brows, grinning up at him.

He swallowed quickly. If she kept smiling at him like that, he was liable to sweep her into his arms, slam his cock into her and fuck her breathless right there in the parking lot.

"It's not that," he denied. He didn't quite trust himself to keep his hands off her if she drove instead of him.

"I was teasing. I have no problem with going in your car."

"Good." He resisted the urge to offer her his arm and they walked to his car together.

In the confines of his car, it was difficult to think of anything other than how close she was and how much he'd like to touch her. *Okay, Rick. Get real. You are not going to take her to bed.* What he needed to do was talk so he wouldn't sit there fantasizing about her. "What kind of music do you like?" he asked

"I like nearly all types of music, but my absolute favorites are blues and mellow jazz. I like to close my eyes and sway to music I can feel through my bones and all the way down to my soul."

He bit back the urge to offer to take her to his favorite jazz club. They spent the rest of the twenty-minute drive to the River Rooms talking about their individual jazz and blues favorites. When they arrived, he held the passenger door open for her and offered her his arm. She gave him a breathtaking smile and slipped her arm through his.

He had to look away to keep from staring down into her cleavage. When they were seated in one of the high backed booths, he made no attempt to look away from her.

After sipping at drinks, they ordered their dinner. Used to women who ordered tiny salads with low-calorie dressing and diet drinks, he listened in amazement as she ordered a salad with regular dressing — to be followed by veal scaloppini.

She clearly enjoyed her food, and he enjoyed watching her savor every bite.

"What sort of things do you like to do?"

She smiled. "I like sitting in jazz clubs, walking barefoot along the beach in the moonlight, dancing on a boat, and sweating to the oldies."

"Sweating to the oldies?"

"You sound surprised. What? You think full-figured gals are all couch potatoes?"

"No," he denied, feeling the heat rise up the back of his neck. "Of course not."

She tilted her head to one side and her thick, dark hair cascaded against one shoulder. She shook her head. "Why don't I believe you?"

"I have no idea," he said wearily.

"Well, this full-figured or size-positive gal works out regularly. All my...parts work perfectly. "

He allowed his gaze to flick briefly over her. Maybe that explained why she seemed so...solid. Granted, she was much larger than any woman he'd ever been out with. Nevertheless, she was as sexy as hell with it, especially her delectable-looking cleavage. A man could probably bury his face between those beautiful peaks and never want to surface again. He felt his cock stirring and shifted uncomfortably in his seat.

"Oh, I'll just bet they do." The comment surprised him and if the arching of her brows were an indicator, her too. "It might interest you to know that all my...parts work rather well, too."

She treated him to one of those delicious smiles of hers and he sighed. Damn, it was going to be a long, frustrating night.

They talked sports over dinner. He found that she was a big baseball and basketball fan.

"No hockey or football?"

She shook her head and swallowed a mouthful of her veal scaloppini. "No, but I have to admit I do occasionally turn on football with no sound."

"Why no sound?"

29

"Well, I'm not really into football."

"Then why watch it?"

"I like watching all those guys with nice tight buns running around." She bit her lip and laughed, a warm, sweet sound that seemed to caress his ears. "I've shocked you."

"No. Believe me, it takes more than that to shock me."

"Then what's that look about?"

"It's just that you're different from any woman I've been out with."

"Size wise?"

"Yes," he admitted, "but that's not the only way you're different." He paused, not sure how to put his thoughts into words. "You're different in a...very nice way."

"Thank you. So are you."

"Me? How?"

She sipped her drink, then ran the tip of her tongue along her bottom lip, an action he found highly erotic. "Well, you're blond, for one thing."

He stared at her. "And?"

"Well, you know what they say about blonds," she said, widening her eyes.

"Being dumb?" he asked, the heat rising up the back of his neck again. "That's what they say about blonde women, not blond men."

"Well, if you say they only mean it for women—" she said, her lips curving in an enchanting smile.

"Are you by any chance implying that I'm a dumb blond?"

"No. I did say you were different, didn't I?"

"So you did."

Both smiling, they finished their main course in silence. He watched as she slowly ate a piece of cheesecake, clearly savoring each bite. It was a nice change to be out with a woman who didn't make him feel like a pig because he wanted something more substantial than a big bowl of lettuce for dinner.

Noticing his close scrutiny, a faint hint of color touched her cheeks. "Would you like a bite?"

About to shake his head, he nodded instead. "Just to see what all the oohing and aahing is about."

She looked around for a clean fork.

"That one will do," he told her.

She held up her fork. "This one?"

"Yes, assuming, of course, you're not poisoned or have a really bad cold."

"No poison or cold germs." She used her fork to offer him a piece of the cheesecake. He leaned forward. She put the fork in his mouth. Their gazes met and locked. He swallowed the small piece of cake without really tasting it.

"So? Do you like it?" Her voice sounded slightly breathless.

"Yes...I like yo — it."

She smiled and looked at him from beneath lowered lids. "I like yo — it too."

He sat back. "Do you mind if I ask your age?"

She shook her head. "Twenty-nine."

"Really? You look younger."

"And do you look younger than you are?"

"I don't know. I'm forty."

"Really?" She widened her eyes. "I would have sworn you weren't a day over thirty-nine years and three hundred and sixty days or so."

They laughed together and he decided she was even prettier when she laughed.

They talked sports for a while longer before he asked her if she'd like to dance.

She nodded and smiled. "Yes. They're playing one of my favorite songs."

He listened and realized the song in question was the instrumental version of Billy Joel's *Just The Way You Are.* "I like it too."

As they danced, she burrowed against him, resting her cheek against his shoulder and moving her hands in small, caressing motions against his back. He found that he liked the weight of her body against his. The feel of her big breasts against his chest caused his cock to slowly come to life. Oh, damn! He drew his lower body away from hers. He hoped she hadn't felt the beginnings of his desire. When she lifted her head and looked up at him, he saw the awareness of his yearning in her gaze.

"I…I'm sorry," he said. "It's been awhile and I…"

"No need to apologize," she told him.

To his amazement, she moved her lower body against his and there was no hiding his growing erection from her. He wasn't in the mood to be teased then sent on his way to take a cold shower.

He dropped his arms and stepped away from her. "Ah, we should go."

She shrugged. "Okay. If that's what you want."

"It's what I need to do."

She sighed. "I've shocked you again. Haven't I? You expected me to be coy or maybe to pretend to be coy?"

Not exactly, but he also hadn't expected her to press against his hardening cock either. "I don't and didn't expect anything in particular. We agreed to spend a few hours together for charity. We've done that."

There was no mistaking the flush on her cheeks. "So we have. Well, let's go."

He knew she'd misunderstood his meaning and probably thought he hadn't enjoyed their evening together. He had, but he decided to let it pass.

At the Fourth Street lot, he insisted on following her in his car to make sure she arrived safely home.

"That's not necessary," she told him, her voice cool.

"Maybe not, but I'd like to…unless you really object."

"No. Fine."

Thirty minutes later, he parked his car behind hers and walked her into her apartment building. They rode the elevator in silence. At her apartment door, they stood staring at each other for several moments before she spoke. "I'm sorry you didn't have a better time."

She sounded shy and a little uncertain. He knew the feeling. He wanted to kiss her, but he didn't want to give her the wrong idea. "What are you talking about? I had a great time."

"You did?"

"Yes. I did."

"Oh, good. So did I."

She smiled that amazing smile of hers that turned her pretty face into a beautiful one. Caution be damned. He had to have at least one chaste kiss before they said goodbye.

He brushed his fingers against her cheek before bending his head. He intended to peck at her mouth briefly, but the moment their lips met, he felt a rush of desire. Fighting to control it, he pressed three quick kisses against her lips before he lifted his head and looked down at her.

She kept her eyes closed for several seconds before looking up at him with her wide silver gaze. He stared back. The hint of red on her cheeks served to make her even more alluring. He wanted another kiss, maybe several more—longer and deeper.

He slipped his hands under the long, dark curtain of her hair to cup her face in his palms. He bent his head slowly, giving her ample time to object. She gave him a shy, sweet smile, closed her eyes, and lifted her face.

He brushed his lips gently against hers, nipped at her mouth until she sucked in a breath and parted her lips. Then he kissed her. Her lips, soft and warm, clung to his. He kissed her hungrily, savoring the taste and texture of her mouth. He sucked at her tongue and slipped an arm around her waist to draw her body against his.

She shivered and leaned closer. He deepened the kiss, moving his hand from her cheek to close his fingers in the long dark hair at the nape of her neck. Her breasts pressing against his chest heightened his desire. With one final long kiss, he reluctantly drew away from her. He was so aroused his cock felt as if it weighed a ton.

She opened her eyes and they silently stared at each other. Her cheeks were flushed, her beautiful silver eyes bright, and her lips still slightly parted. He wondered if she, like he, wanted the kissing to go on and on until it went beyond the kissing stage. And that would not do. He'd had a surprisingly great time with her and done his bit for charity. Now it was time to get the hell out of there before he lost his head completely.

"Would you like to come in for coffee?"

The question didn't surprise him nearly as much as his instinctive desire to seize the opportunity to get her alone behind closed doors and maybe into bed. After her eager response to his kisses, he had a feeling she might be receptive to allowing him to spend the night. With his cock hardening at an alarming rate, he longed to take her to bed. He gazed into her eyes again and saw a complete lack of guile. She was different from the women he was used to bedding, who thought nothing of hopping into bed for a one-nighter and moving on without a single backward glance.

He smiled. "Thanks, but I'd better hit the road."

Her smile wavered for a moment before she widened it. She extended her hand. "Goodbye."

He enclosed her hand in both of his. The surge of desire he felt was so strong he dropped her hand and took several steps away from her. "Goodbye."

* * * * *

The soft jazz filling the car as Rick drove home kept thoughts of Jennifer uppermost in his mind. He couldn't stop thinking about her or their evening together. Recalling her response to his touch and kisses made his cock throb. What the hell had possessed him to turn down her invitation for "coffee"? It wasn't as if he'd pressured her in anyway. She had freely extended the invitation he'd so badly wanted to accept. Just maybe she needed or wanted some cock. And damn it! He needed some pussy.

Halfway home, he decided he'd made a big mistake. She was an adult. If she wanted him to spend the night with her, why shouldn't he? With visions of her beautiful face and silver eyes spurring him on, he got off the highway at the next exit and turned his car around.

* * * * *

Well, no nookie for you tonight, Jennifer thought as she closed her apartment door. She undressed quickly, tossing the two-piece dress in a heap on her bedroom floor. *A lot of help you were.* She put on her sexiest nightgown, one made of sheer black silk and lace that showcased her breasts and ended halfway up her thighs. She made herself a cup of decaffeinated tea, got into bed, and called Cherica.

"So. How did it go?"

She sipped her tea and lay back against her pillow. "I'm alone."

"Oh. Why didn't you invite him in?"

"I did...he declined."

"He did? Why?"

Cherica sounded so surprised. She smiled. "Well, maybe he doesn't go for big gals."

"You think?"

She recalled the feel of his cock hardening against her. "I guess. He turned down my invitation to come in."

"Well, that's his loss."

"Yeah." She sighed. "But I was so hoping to get laid tonight."

"I know the feeling," Cherica said and they both laughed.

"So what about you? When are you and Maurice hitting the town?"

"Saturday night. God, I hope I have better luck," Cherica said and they dissolved into fresh peals of laughter.

"Well, I know you have an early day tomorrow, so I'll say goodnight."

"Goodnight," Cherica echoed.

Jennifer finished her tea, turned off her bedroom light, and settled down to sleep. She thought briefly of Rick. Too bad he'd turned out to be a blond tease. He'd stared at her cleavage all night, held her close as they'd slow danced, kissed the lipstick off her mouth, got her all hot and bothered, and then decided he had no interest in doing anything about it. Oh, yeah, he was a tease all right.

She was just becoming drowsy when the phone by her bed rang. She sat up and reached for the receiver. "Hello?"

"Hi. Were you asleep?"

It took her a moment to recognize the voice. "Ah, no...who...Rick?"

"Yes. I was halfway home when I realized that I wanted a cup of coffee after all, but I don't have any coffee at home. I was wondering if your coffee invitation was still open."

"Ah...sure...if you want to stop by in the morning for coffee...sure."

"Actually, I meant now. Tonight. I'm in your lobby."

"You are?"

"Yes. May I come up?"

Her heart began to thump. "Ah...sure...ah...yeah...I'll buzz you in."

"Thank you."

She released the door buzzer and hung up. She turned on the light and scrambled out of bed. She glanced wildly around for something to throw over her sheer, revealing gown. She generally didn't use a dressing gown, but she couldn't very well open the door with her breasts so clearly visible.

With her hand on an old gown she found at the back of her closet, she froze. Why was she scrambling to find something to cover her gown with? She hadn't intended to give him coffee when she'd invited him in earlier and he hadn't decided to come back for coffee. He'd come back because he wanted to spend the night with her—or at least an hour or two.

Still, she didn't want to look too eager to get laid. She slipped the short, battered dressing gown on and hurried through the apartment as her doorbell sounded.

Pausing long enough to rake her hands through her hair as she passed the mirror in the small foyer, she took a deep breath. "Yes?"

"It's Rick."

She bit her lip. *Oh, God!* Did she want to do this? She'd never had a one-night stand. Wasn't she a little old to start sowing wild oats?

"Jennifer?"

It was a little late to start second-guessing herself. He was there now, at her invitation. Besides, she wanted sex. Tonight. She removed the chains and the locks from the door and stepped back.

He smiled and extended a box of chocolates and a bouquet of flowers to her. "Hi again."

"Hi. Thank you." She took his offerings and placed them on the table near the door. "Where did you get these?"

"I passed a 24 hour flower shop and I thought the chocolates would go good with the coffee."

Okay, it was now or she'd lose her nerve. She licked her lips and gave him a nervous smile. "Actually, I just realized that I don't have any coffee in the house..."

Their gazes met and locked. She saw clear desire in his blue-green eyes. She made no effort to hide her own longing.

"Oh. In that case, I'll settle for a couple of kisses."

"Well...actually, I was hoping you'd want a little more than a few kisses." As she spoke, she slowly opened her dressing gown.

His gaze moved slowly over her body before locking with hers again. "I want a lot more than a few kisses, but I think we should probably understand each other before we go any further," he said.

Okay, here's where he tells me he just wants a 'slam bam thank you ma'am fuck.' "Meaning?"

"Meaning I would really like to spend the night with you, but...I'm not looking for a relationship."

She shook her head. "What you really mean is that you're not ready for a relationship with a fat gal, but that's okay because I'm not looking for a relationship with you, Blondie. All I want from you tonight is some cock. Can you accommodate me?" Her cheeks burned and she averted her gaze.

He tipped a finger under her chin to encourage her to look up at him again. "Yes. I can accommodate you tonight, but please don't call me Blondie."

"Okay. Do you...are you...did you come prepared?" She glanced away again. "Do you need to go back out...for...anything?"

"I'm prepared. We don't need to do anything accept make love to each other," he said and eased the dressing gown off her shoulders.

She felt a surge of feminine satisfaction when he drew in a sharp breath as he looked at her. She felt her nipples harden under the prolonged gaze he allowed to linger on her breasts.

"You...you're...God, I want to touch you..." He cupped her face between his palms and began raining warm kisses against her mouth and her throat. His lips and his hands touching and caressing her invoked feelings she'd kept on a tight rein for months. Now she allowed herself to enjoy being touched and kissed. And when she felt his cock coming to life, she went damp between her legs.

She linked her arms around his neck. As she returned his kisses, she deliberately rotated her lower body against his. Still raining kisses over her face and throat, he slipped a hand down her body over her stomach. She shivered and parted her legs. He eased first one finger, then another into her pussy, sending a chill through her body.

He bent his head and took the tip of her right breast between his lips. He gently finger fucked her while he sucked and tongued her nipple through the sheer material of the gown. She felt as if she were floating. It had been so long since anyone had made love to her, and this felt so good. She moaned and eagerly thrust her left breast into his mouth when he released the right one.

By the time he lifted his head and stepped away from her, her pussy pulsed with need and moisture. He reached down and lifted her gown over her head and tossed it aside.

She stood before him, naked and more than a little apprehensive. She knew she had large breasts and big, long legs, but her stomach had an alarming swell and her behind was probably way more padded and flabby than any he'd ever seen. She knew her full-figured body was a lot different from the bodies of slender-hipped women he was probably used to bedding.

He reached out a hand and touched her breasts. He glided his hand down her body, over her stomach to her mound. He felt around until he touched her clit, sending a flash of heat all through her.

"You're beautiful," he said and began pulling his clothes off.

She swallowed quickly and then bit her lip when he stood naked and aroused before her. His body was like a work of art. It was taut and muscular. He had wide shoulders, a nice chest covered with dark blond hair that flowed down his body, breaking off just before reaching his narrow hips. His cock jutted out from a tangle of dark, curly hair.

Her pussy pulsed as she looked at his cock. It was as beautiful as the rest of his body. To her delight, it was thick and hard with a big, pink head that would plow though her aching pussy, bringing nothing but pleasure. God, but she wanted that lovely piece of flesh inside her.

Catching her breath, she lifted her gaze to his face, her lips slightly parted.

Correctly interpreting her needs, he took her into his arms and rubbed against her. She shuddered and clung to him, moaning softly.

"Let's go to bed," he told her softly.

"Yes, oh God, yes!"

He bent to remove several small foil packages from his pocket. She took his hand and led him into her bedroom. He eased her down onto the side of the bed. He tossed several condoms onto the night table and handed her one. Her hands trembled as she opened the packet. He moved closer and she began to cover his cock with the condom.

She did it slowly, almost loathing to cover his beautiful shaft. Just for one wild moment she imagined how thrilling it would be to feel his naked dick sliding into her bare, unprotected pussy. The thought sent a fresh rush of moisture down into her already soaked passage.

With the rubber inplace, she lay back on the bed and gave his cock a little tug to encourage him. He bent and kissed her gently as he eased his big body down on top of hers. He was heavy, and she luxuriated in his weight pressing down on her. She shifted her body as best she could in an attempt to part her legs.

He lifted his lower body slightly, and she opened her legs and reached for his cock. While he rested his weight on his extended arms, she slowly rubbed his shaft up and down the length of her pussy. Finally, she jerked her hips up against his. She closed her eyes and gasped softly when he lowered his body back onto hers. She felt the head of his cock slip into her vagina.

He pushed slowly and steadily into her until he was fully seated within. Then he lifted her chin and pressed his mouth against her lips. She shuddered and slipped her arms around his body, stroking her hands down his back and over his buns. They lay fully and tightly joined for several moments, their lower bodies motionless as they exchanged slow, hungry kisses that gradually built in intensity.

His motionless dick felt good inside of her, but she needed more. She tightened her inner muscles around him and lifted her hips in several quick movements. He withdrew slightly, and then began to thrust into her with a deliciously languid motion that sent waves of heat out from her pussy right down to her curled toes. Oh, lord, that felt good! Whoever said size didn't matter must not have known the absolute, mind-boggling pleasure of having a thick, hard, amorous man sliding in and out of her.

She closed her eyes and clung to him, rotating her hips and lifting her body up to meet his downward thrusts. Every time he bottomed out in her, a small sigh of pleasure escaped her parted lips—until he began kissing her. Then she could only moan into his open mouth. When he sucked on her tongue, she felt her pussy creaming around his thick shaft and the muscles in her stomach began clenching. Oh, God, she was getting ready to come.

He broke their lip lock and showered her face and neck with kisses. Just as she felt her passion spiraling out of control, he closed his lips over her right breast. He reached between their bodies and began rubbing a thumb against her clit. She exploded, coming in a fast, furious rush that obliterated everything but the most elemental feelings and needs. There was just him and the wonderful, thick cock sending her straight to fantasyland.

He continued to suck her breast and slowly slid in and out of her now-drenched channel as she shuddered and moaned. Finally, when her senses settled down, he lifted her chin and began kissing her again. She sighed, stroking her hands down his back. She could feel his body tightening and shaking and she knew he was about to come.

She sucked on his tongue and raked her hands over his clenching buns until he drove his cock into her in a series of rough, short thrusts that finally culminated in his coming. He pushed into her so hard it hurt, and collapsed on top of her, shuddering and groaning, with his face against her neck.

She stroked his back and kissed his hair, relishing the weight of his big, sweaty body on hers. God, it felt good to have a man lying on top of her with a hard, thick cock buried balls deep in her very satisfied pussy.

After several moments, he turned his head and found her mouth. They exchanged a long, heated kiss before he groaned and pulled out of her. He discarded the condom and rolled onto his side with his body pressed against hers. She turned onto her side and cuddled her body against his.

They began kissing again, then caressing each other. In a matter of minutes, he was hard again. She caressed his cock and pushed him onto his back. She quickly rolled a condom over his dick before slowly impaling herself on him.

"Oh, damn!" He grabbed her hips and held her body pressed tightly against his, as he eagerly shoved his dick deep up into her pussy.

She moaned and fell forward, burying her face against his shoulder. "Oooh! Oh, don't stop. Harder! Please. Push it in harder and faster!"

"I have no intentions of stopping until my dick goes limp." Wrapping his arms around her waist, he rolled them over until she lay on her back and he was above her, between her legs. Resting most of his weight on his extended arms, he began to hammer at her pussy with a force and passion that quickly pushed her into one of the sweetest and most overwhelming orgasms of her life.

She clutched him to her, greedily thrusting her pussy up to receive his raging cock. Wave after wave of bliss buffeted her body. She cried out and bit into his shoulder, her pussy spasming wildly.

"Oh, damn! Damn. Here it comes, baby!"

His climax, which shook his whole body, quickly followed hers. He collapsed onto her with his lips brushing her neck. "Oh, man! That was so damned good."

With her eyes closed, she smiled and raked her fingers lazily down his back. "Not bad for a blond guy," she told him, her voice soft and slurred with the remnants of desire.

He laughed and brushed his lips against hers. "Yeah? Well, from your response, I can only conclude that you like blond guys," he told her.

"I can't stand blond guys," she countered, curled her fingers in his hair, and pressed a scorching kiss against his lips.

"Oh, yeah, I can tell that," he told her when they came up for air from the kiss.

He was still inside her and she liked that. God, she loved a man who lingered in her pussy after coming. "It's late," she whispered. "Will you spend the rest of the night with me?"

"Oh, yeah!" He kissed her again and began easing his cock out of her body.

She pressed her lips together to keep from crying out in protest. It had been so long since she'd made love and she was loath to have him remove his cock. She told herself she was being greedy but she was hard-pressed not to clamp her pussy muscles down in an attempt to keep his cock inside her.

He urged her onto her side and curled his body against her back.

She drew the cover up over their bodies and fell asleep with one of his hands cupping at her breasts. She smiled sleepily. There was nothing quite as nice as having a man in her bed again.

Chapter Four

Rick stood by the bed, looking down at Jennifer as she slept. She lay on her stomach with her dark hair covering her face. Although he'd pulled a light sheet up over her shoulders when he slipped out of bed, the generous curves of her body were clearly outlined to his gaze.

In the light of morning with his desire sated, he could see all the imperfections in her body that had not concerned him the night before. Her hips were wide, her bottom neither firm nor taut, and her inner thighs were bigger than any he'd ever seen on a woman. Her breasts were not as pert as he'd imagined in the heat of passion. Every woman he'd ever slept with had possessed a much more attractive body. So why the hell was he becoming aroused just looking at her?

He ran a hand through his hair. It was nearly six-thirty. He needed to finish dressing and leave. He sighed. What he really wanted was to climb back into bed with her. Thoughts of their night together awakened his desire. He glanced at the nightstand. The sight of the lone condom made his cock ache. He shook his head and turned away. He retrieved his shirt and jacket from the living room floor and finished dressing.

With his hand on the apartment door, he paused. Leaving while she was asleep smacked of cowardice. The last thing he wanted was for her to wake and regret their night together. He turned away from the door and went in search of the kitchen.

Forty-five minutes later, he carried a loaded breakfast tray into the bedroom. He put the tray on the dresser and sat on the side of the bed. He leaned down and brushed her hair aside. He kissed her shoulders and neck. Imperfect body or not, she had

45

given him one of the most satisfying nights of his love life. He had enjoyed making love to her more than any woman in recent memory.

He wanted to make love to her again. He glanced at the condom on the nightstand. *One more time,* he thought. He pressed his lips against her neck and caressed her shoulders. "Hey," he said softly.

After a moment, she began to stir. She rolled onto her back, revealing her breasts. He sucked in a breath. Okay, so they weren't the perfect silicon spheres he was used to. They had felt good against his face and tasted sweet in his mouth.

Her eyes fluttered open. A slow, engaging smile touched her lips.

He bent and kissed her mouth. When she returned his kiss and stroked her fingers through his hair, he knew he had to have her again. "What time do you have to be at work?"

"I...I don't...I work from home." She ran her tongue along the outline of his mouth. "What about you?"

"I'll get there when I get there."

She gently sank her teeth into his bottom lip. "What did you have in mind?"

"A mini repeat of last night." He caressed her cheek. "Is that possible?"

"I smell food."

"I cooked you breakfast. Home fries, eggs, and toast."

"It sounds and smells too good to waste," she teased.

"You can eat it later."

She stroked her hands across his shoulders. "You're all dressed."

"I can easily remedy that." He stood up and quickly disrobed.

She licked her lips and smiled shyly as her gaze centered on his semi-erect cock. Her mixture of eagerness and shyness was a huge turn on. He bent and kissed her lips quickly before he pulled the cover off her and pressed his body against hers on the bed.

He fondled her big, warm breasts and rubbed his lower body against hers as they shared long, exploring kisses. Minutes later, his cock was fully erect and he was fighting the urge to roll her onto her back and sink his aching dick deep inside her. The hardening tips of her tits against his palms excited his already heightened passions. An exploring finger dipped into her pussy told him that she wasn't quite ready to receive his cock.

He continued to kiss and caress her, whispering to her. He inserted a finger inside her and gently began to finger fuck her. She moaned.

"You like that?" he asked.

She tossed her head from side to side in response, causing her breasts to jiggle enticingly against his chest. He bent his head and greedily took the tip of one sweet globe into his mouth.

As he sucked and fingered her, she began shuddering and he realized she'd just had a mini orgasm. His finger was bathed in her warm juices. She was now as ready as he was. He withdrew his finger and quickly rolled away. He donned the lone condom on the nightstand and rejoined her on the bed.

She parted her big, beautiful thighs, reaching for his cock with both hands. He settled between her legs and pressed the head of his dick against her entrance. She pushed up her hips and he slipped inside her. Oh, damn, but she felt so good...warm, moist, and tight. Oh, damn, she had good pussy.

He was immediately lost in her sweetness. Her lips teased, her breasts pleased, her pussy thrilled and inundated his senses with unbelievable pleasure. His half-formed plan to make their last time together last was quickly blown away. It was all he could do not to explode prematurely inside her. His body tensed with the effort of holding back his release.

She stroked her soft, warm hands down his back and pushed her hips up to swallow him as he propelled his throbbing dick down into her pussy. Oh, shit! She didn't seem to be ready, but he knew he couldn't hold on much longer. His nuts felt as if they were about to burst.

"It's all right," she whispered blowing gently into his ear. "Go ahead. Come. Explode." To enforce her command, she tightened her pussy around his cock and clutched at his ass.

He lost it. He lay his body on hers, flattening her breasts under his chest, and blew his load into her. To his relief, he felt her pussy clenching involuntarily around his dick as he pumped the last few drops of his seed out of his cock. Oh, damn. She was sweet.

Breathing deeply, he settled against her. He liked the fact that he didn't have to roll off of her almost immediately after lovemaking for fear of crushing her. It was nice to know that she could bear his weight, at least for a time. She seemed to enjoy having him on top of her. They touched and kissed each other briefly. Then he lay with his face against her neck, her big breasts squashed under his chest, his cock still inside her.

Damn this was nice. He hated the thought of getting up and leaving her. A sudden desire to pull out of her, disgard the condom, and slide back into her was alluring. Talk about delusional thinking. There was no way he would ever make love to a woman he hadn't known for years and been in a committed relationship without the benefit of one of his trusty rubbers between them.

Lying on top of her was filling his head with insane ideas. He needed to get the hell up and out of there. He gave her neck a long last kiss and reluctantly withdrew his cock from her pussy. She muttered in protest and clutched briefly at his shoulders. Rolling onto his side, he discarded the condom. Then he lay on his back, staring up at the ceiling. He wanted to talk to her, but he felt awkward. He should have left while she was asleep.

But then he would have missed the sweet, early morning treat they'd just shared. He rolled onto his side and propped himself up on his elbow. Gazing down into her face, he was struck anew by how very beautiful she was. "You are so sweet."

She smiled. What he wouldn't give for just one more rubber. It had been a long time since a feminine smile had made his dick stir this way. He wanted her again.

"This is...ah...I have to go," he told her.

Twin red spots appeared on her cheeks. She yanked the cover up over her bare breasts. "I don't see anyone keeping you here against your will."

"I...ah...look...that didn't come out as I'd intended, but...this is awkward."

"It doesn't need to be." Even as she spoke, he could see the discomfort in her gaze, hear it in her voice. "We both agreed that we wanted to sleep together. Well, we have. You don't need to worry that I'll expect a repeat performance. Last night and this morning was...you're obviously not really into big women and I'm not into blonds. "

He stared down at her. How the hell did she know what type of women he was into? He wanted to say something...anything to relieve the sudden tension between them, but what could he say? "I...ah...I'm going to shower and go."

She nodded silently. She shifted onto her stomach with her face turned away from him. "Go."

He balled his hand into a fist to keep from touching her. It didn't help. He dropped a quick kiss against the back of her neck.

"Don't," she said. "Just go. Okay?"

Half an hour later he was in his car and on his way home to change before he headed to the office late. Normally, after a night of satisfying lovemaking, he felt relaxed and upbeat. After leaving Jennifer, he felt restless and uneasy. He knew he could have handled their parting better. How? He wasn't quite sure, but this way felt all wrong. To just walk away and leave her huddled under the covers with an impersonal goodbye seemed tacky and unkind. He frowned. They had both gotten what they'd wanted, a hot night of fucking. There was no need for wallowing in regrets or for him to feel that he had behaved badly. Nevertheless, he picked up his car phone and ordered flowers for her.

When asked what the card should say, he said simply. "Just...Rick. Nothing else."

* * * * *

"You're very quiet. Are you upset by last night?"

Jennifer cast a brief, startled glance at Cherica who walked about a foot from her. Twice a week, she and Cherica donned running shoes and sweats and hit the track at one of the local colleges for a class on power walking.

"Why should I be upset?"

"Well, you know...because he chose not to stay."

She walked on in silence for several moments. Then she shook her head. Her reluctance to talk about her night with Rick surprised her. She and Cherica had been best friends since junior high. They had never kept secrets from each other. She wasn't going to start now.

"We had a great time at dinner," she said slowly. "We like a lot of the same things."

"Hmm. "

Her cheeks burned as she remembered the previous night and that morning. "After I talked to you last night, he called me and asked if he could come back."

"What?!" Cherica put a hand on her arm and they both stopped so abruptly that the walkers behind them had to swerve to avoid bumping into them.

"Okay, ladies, let's keep it moving," the instructor called from the rear of the double line of walkers. "This is power walking, not power standing."

Exchanging grins, she and Cherica began moving again.

"And you said?"

"I said yes and we spent the night together."

"And did he...disappoint?"

"No. He's a...no, he didn't disappoint."

"Had a...nice time, did ya?"

"Very nice," she said, the corners of her lips twitching.

"Sooo?"

"Sooo what?"

"So when are you seeing each other again?"

She shook her head. "I'm not. It was very nice, but it was a one-nighter. That's what we both agreed on."

"And you're okay with that?"

To her surprise, she was. Sure, there was a part of her that wondered what a relationship with him might have been like, but the more practical part of her knew that just wasn't going to happen. Although they had several shared interests and were sexually compatible, she wasn't his type. She had learned the hard way that men with blond hair had been created for one purpose: to break her heart.

"Yes."

"Well, I'm not so sure I buy that you are...in any case, he's a dumb blond," Cherica fumed.

Jennifer laughed. "Come on, Rica. He was totally upfront with me *before* we hit the sack. If nothing else, he's honest. You gotta respect an honest man." She hesitated before going on. "He cooked me breakfast before he left and sent me flowers after he had."

"Breakfast in bed, huh?"

She nodded. "Well, sort of. We sort of...had another go-round this morning before he left and then I warmed it up and ate it alone."

"Another go-round?"

She nodded. "He's a...great in bed."

"Ah huh. What kind of flowers did he send?"

"A very elegant mixed bouquet." She laughed. "He was probably afraid to send roses."

"What did the card say?"

"Nothing. He just had his name signed. I think it was his way of reinforcing the idea that what we had was a one-night stand and nothing more."

Cherica grunted.

"What about you? Looking forward to your date with Maurice?"

"Yes."

Cherica's voice sounded forced and she glanced quickly at her profile: resolute. She was determined to enjoy her date. She had a feeling Cherica would have sounded much more excited if she'd had a date with Jayson planned for Saturday night, but she remained silent. Cherica would just have to come to terms with her real feelings for Jayson in her own time. Hopefully, that would happen *before* Jayson met someone else and was lost to Cherica forever.

"Come on, ladies…pick up the pace…double-time for the last quarter mile," the instructor called out.

They doubled their pace and finished the rest of the walk in silence.

* * * * *

"Are you feeling okay?"

Rick smiled at Angie, sitting across the kitchen table from him. "I'm feeling fine. Why do you ask?"

"You've hardly said two words since you arrived and even Sherri hasn't managed to chase that gloomy look off your face for long. What's wrong?"

He put down the sandwich he'd only taken a few bites from and sighed. Maybe dropping everything at work and rushing over to Troy and Angie's house uninvited in the middle of the day hadn't been such a good idea. But he'd needed to talk and

Troy was too overwhelmed with a new client to be interrupted. As the managing partner of Hunter and Markham, Rick spent most of his work day handling the everyday problems every business encountered, which left Troy and their small staff to handle the actual software designing end of the business.

During the last two years, he'd discovered that Angie was easy to talk to. She was never judgmental and always willing to listen. Even when she didn't have any useful advice to offer, he found just talking to her soothing.

Not that he was about to tell her of the one-night stand he'd had with Jennifer. "I'm just feeling a little...I think it's time I settled down." He smiled at her. "I want what Troy has...a beautiful, adoring wife and a kid or two."

"So get married. You're a good-looking guy with a lot to offer a woman. You are not going to have any problem finding a woman to love and cherish you and have your babies." She tilted her head to one side and looked at him. "Have anyone in mind?"

A sudden image of Jennifer's face intruded on his consciousness. He frowned and pushed it away. She was beautiful, sweet, and passionate, but she was not his type. Now Carolyn was his type and she was probably just as sweet and passionate as Jennifer. She was certainly just as attractive. Actually, she was more attractive.

"Yes."

She smiled and leaned her chin on her palms. "Tell me about her."

"She's beautiful and..."

"And slender and blond?" she prodded when he trailed off.

"Yes," he said quickly, dismayed that he had been about to say dark and full-figured. Even if he had wanted to see Jennifer again, she had made it plain what she thought of blond men.

"When do I get to meet her?"

He shook his head, smiling. "It's way too early for that. I've only seen her once."

"But you liked what you saw?"

"Yes."

"So do you have a date with her?" She frowned at him. "Work with me here, Rick. Don't make me pull teeth."

He laughed. "Actually, I'm going to call her when I get back to work and ask her out."

"That's the spirit. Wine her and dine her and sweep her off her feet."

"Yeah. That was the plan."

"And when you're sure she's the right one, or even if you're not sure, bring her by for a meal. I'd love to meet her and tell her what a great guy you are."

He got up and went around the table to kiss her cheek. "Thanks, sweets."

She smiled up at him. "Anytime you need to talk, Rick, I'm here."

He nodded. "I know and I appreciate it." He kissed her cheek again. "Well, I'm going to go up to Sherri's room to kiss her goodbye, then I'm heading back to work."

"Okay. I'll wrap up your sandwich and meet you at the front door."

On his way back to work, he called Carolyn on his car phone and asked her to have dinner with him.

"I'd love to have dinner with you," she told him in a sultry voice that stirred his cock and his imagination. "When did you have in mind?"

"I know it's short notice, but I'd love to take you to dinner this Saturday."

"Saturday is fine," she told him.

He smiled. He liked her lack of guile and the way she didn't try to pretend she had to check her calendar to see if she were free. "Great. What time can I pick you up?"

"How does six sound?"

"Fine. What's your address?"

She gave him directions to her apartment, which was on the opposite side of the city from his house. "Fine. I'll see you Saturday at six," he told her.

"I was hoping you'd call. I'm looking forward to seeing you."

"And I you."

"Bye."

"Until Saturday."

Feeling better and looking forward to getting to know the beautiful Carolyn, he whistled softly. By the time he arrived back at the office, his mood had brightened considerably and he quickly settled down to work. Occasional thoughts of Jennifer flashed in his head, but he resolutely dismissed them. No use longing for a woman who didn't want a real relationship with him. He had a feeling she wouldn't be adverse to their becoming part-time lovers. Having made up his mind it was time to settle down, he reluctantly acknowledged that one-night stands, no matter how hot, had to go.

Chapter Five

Jennifer tossed aside the glossy magazine she'd had open to the same page for a good fifteen minutes. She looked at her watch. It was just five-thirty. She felt restless and disgruntled. This was no way to spend a Saturday night. She picked up the TV remote and began channel surfing. She'd cycled through all the available channels twice when her phone buzzed, signaling that someone was in the lobby to see her.

She lowered the sound on the TV and picked up phone. "Hello?"

"Hi, beautiful."

She immediately recognized the male voice and smiled. "Hi yourself, handsome."

"I'm in the lobby. Can I come up?"

"Of course." She released the lobby door and rose to her feet.

"You look great," he told her in the soft, deep voice she'd always loved, when she admitted him.

She allowed her gaze to flick over him. He was just over six feet tall with smooth skin the color of cocoa and dark, liquid brown eyes. He was a big, attractive man who reeked of sex appeal. As always, when she looked at him, she was amazed that some woman hadn't snatched him up a long time ago.

In a dark suit with a matching silk tie, he looked as if he were ready for a night on the town. "You're looking pretty good yourself," she said, slipping her arm through his. "You have a date?"

He frowned. "No…I was sort of hoping Rica would want to have dinner with me, but she's not home, apparently. I thought she might be with you."

Jennifer gave an inward sigh. Men. After weeks of practically ignoring Cherica, Jayson would decide he wanted to take her out on the very night she went out with Maurice.

"Nope."

"Where is she?" He frowned. "Is she…seeing someone? Is she out on a date?"

"A date?" She shrugged. "There's an idea. That's what I need—a date. You're all dressed up with no place to go. How about I get dressed up and you take me out? Pretty please? Now I know I'm a poor sub for Rica, but surely I'm better than nothing."

Although he treated her to a charming smile, she could see clear disappointment in his eyes. "I'd be delighted to take you out and you're not a poor substitute for anyone," he said gallantly.

She showered quickly and donned a silk dress with a black bodice, thin straps and a black and rose floral skirt. The v-neckline provided just a hint of cleavage and the skirt fluttered around her calves. Studying her reflection, she decided she would do.

"Wow. You look great," Jayson told her when she waltzed into the living room.

She smiled at him. "You're a doll, Jay. Where are we going? Never mind. Surprise me."

Jayson took her to a popular jazz club on the waterfront. Over dinner, she kept up a nearly non-stop conversation that gave him very little chance to ask her again if Cherica was out with another man that night.

It was as they finished dinner that she glanced up and noticed Rick sitting at another table across the large, dimly lit room. Her gaze moved to his companion—a slender blonde. He looked up suddenly and their gazes met and locked briefly before she looked away.

"Jenn? Something wrong?"

She shook her head and blinked at Jayson. "No. No. I just...I'm going to go freshen up."

In the ladies room, she stared at her reflection. Her face looked washed out and her eyes wide. She looked like one unhappy camper. And why? Because she'd seen a man she'd never expected to see again with a beautiful, slender blonde. A man she cared nothing about, she reminded herself.

She powered her nose, freshened her lipstick, and left the ladies room. She came to an abrupt halt because Rick leaned against a wall a few feet from the exit. She stared at him and then glanced back at the door she'd just exited. "You're waiting for your date. I didn't notice her inside, but would you like me to go back in and check?"

"Thanks, but no. She's not in there."

"Then why are you out here?"

He shrugged and slipped his hands into his trouser pockets. "I was hoping to have a word with you."

"You were? Why?"

"I just wanted to say hello."

"Oh. Hi," she said and started pass him.

He sighed and moved to step in front of her. "Wait a minute, Jennifer."

"What?"

"How are you?"

"Fine. How are you?"

"Okay. Ah, I see you're dating."

"So are you, apparently."

"No. We...she and I are not..."

"Not what? Dating? Sure looks like it from here. She's the blonde from the charity auction. Lucky her." She started pass him.

He put his hand on her arm and she hated that her heart thumped. "What?"

"What do you mean?"

"You said you weren't a dumb blond. It should be obvious."

"Well, it's not."

"I had to spend five hundred dollars for the privilege of spending a night with you. Apparently she gets to do it because she's beautiful, blonde, and slender."

She knew she sounded catty and bitter, but she didn't care. After all, it was the truth. She shook his hand off her arm and walked past him.

He followed her. "Jennifer, wait a minute. Please. You have the wrong idea."

She turned to face him. "I don't think so, Rick."

"Yes, you do. Okay, so she's slender, blonde, and beautiful." He shrugged. "Jennifer, you are beautiful too."

"Really? Well, apparently it's not enough. I need to be slender and blonde not to have to pay for the privilege of spending a few hours with you. Tell me, Rick, will you be spending the night with her too?"

His gaze narrowed and he shook his head. "This is ridiculous. I came to say hello, not to listen to a bunch of crap."

She nodded. "You're right. This is a bunch of crap."

She turned and walked away. She didn't pause or stop when he called out to her. She made her way back to the table where Jayson waited for her.

He rose and put his arm around her. "Hi again, beautiful."

When she glanced past Jayson and saw Rick's eyes narrow and his lips compress into a thin line, she could have kissed Jayson. She settled for slipping an arm around his waist and smiling up at him. "Hello yourself, handsome."

Her glee was short-lived. She shouldn't care what Rick thought about anything. And making him jealous should have been the last thing on her mind. They'd had a date and a night and morning of passion. Period. She'd seen what type of woman he preferred and she didn't qualify. Rather than being jealous, he probably thought she was easy. Her cheeks burned at the thought. To hell with him and what he thought.

* * * * *

"So," Carolyn said into the silence of the car. "How was she?"

Rick kept his gaze on the highway ahead.

"How was who?"

"Your date."

"What date? You're my date and you were fine."

"Thanks," she said dryly. "But I meant your date for the charity auction."

His hands tightened on the steering wheel. "My date for the...what about her?"

"Well, that was her back there at the jazz club."

It wasn't a question and he knew a denial would be useless. Besides, he had no reason to deny it. "Yes," he said briefly.

"So what was she like?"

"I did my bit, she did her bit. Charity benefited."

"I feel your pain."

He felt the back of his neck burning. Damn. Was it that obvious that seeing Jennifer with another man had snatched his joy out of the evening? "What pain?" he asked wearily.

"You're probably too much of a gentleman to admit it, but that must have been the date from hell."

His eyes narrowed. "How the hell did you reach that conclusion?"

"Well, come on, Rick. I guess she's not exactly plain, if you can get pass all that weight. She needs to learn when to push herself away from the table and get out and exercise. And do something with her hair and makeup. Until she drops some of that weight, she'll be getting all of her dates at charity auctions. I hope she has a good job."

She laughed. The laughter he'd found so titillating earlier now irritated the hell out of him. He was sorely tempted to remind her that she had also been at the charity auction bidding on men. Did that mean she needed help getting a man?

"I don't foresee her having anymore problem getting another date than you'll have."

"What?" She made small choking sound. "Surely you're not comparing me to her."

"Why not?"

"Why not?! You can't possibly be serious."

"Oh, but I am. You're both beautiful women."

"We are nothing alike, Rick!"

"No," he agreed quietly. Somehow he didn't think Jennifer was half the bitch Carolyn so clearly was. "I meant it as a compliment," he said, his voice cool. "And in case you missed the obvious, she already has a man. Didn't you notice the guy on her arm?"

"Yeah...that was surprising. He was very good looking too." The car was filled with her annoying laughter again. "Obviously she's been at another charity auction."

How could anyone who was so beautiful be such a bitch? He compressed his lips into a tight line and they made the remainder of the drive in silence.

At her apartment door, she linked her arms around his neck and planted a warm, deep kiss against his lips. He brushed his mouth against hers and drew back.

She smiled up at him. "You'll come in."

From the moment he'd picked her up and saw the stunning blue dress that clung to her body, emphasizing every inch of her, he'd wondered what his chances were of spending the night with her. He'd anticipated that he'd spend the night making love to her. Now thoughts of how bitchy she was turned him off. Jennifer was sweet and guileless and didn't deserve the cattiness this woman had directed at her.

"Thanks, but I'd better pass."

The confident smile on her face wavered. "Ah...you don't want to come in?"

"Actually, I do," he admitted. "But it's late and I'd better go."

She stared up at him. "Ah...you'll call me?"

He hesitated. "I'm sure we'll talk again." He pecked her cheek and walked away.

He thought about Jennifer as he drove home. Was she still with the other man? Was she even now allowing him to make love to her as she'd allowed him to do? His stomach muscles tightened. The thought of her kissing another man, allowing another man to hold and touch her, made the breath catch in his throat. Was she accepting another cock into the pussy that had been so warm and welcoming to his?

Even now, Jennifer and the man might be embarking on a long, uninterrupted night of love. Well, it might be long, but it damn sure wouldn't be uninterrupted, he thought angrily. He reached for his cell phone and dialed her number. There was no answer and he broke the connection after allowing it to ring seven times.

Damn! They were already too engrossed in each other for her to answer the damned phone. At home, he ripped his clothes off and took a cool shower, his thoughts still on Jennifer. He fell into bed and lay staring up at the ceiling.

He was a first class fool. Instead of making passionate love to a willing Carolyn, he was lying there tormented by thoughts of Jennifer and the other man making love. He was probably caressing her big beautiful breasts, eliciting soft moans from her, and making her come.

He rolled over onto his stomach and punched a fist into his pillow. Damn. What the hell was wrong with him? Why was he obsessing over a woman he'd spent one night and morning with? She'd clearly already moved on and forgotten him. What he needed to do was forget her.

He finally fell asleep only to wake an hour or so later with thoughts of Jennifer again haunting him. If the man was another one-night stand, there was nothing to prevent him from calling her and asking her out for a date. A real date this time. He'd wine and dine her, but he wouldn't try to spend the night with her. He'd show her that she was wrong about him and the type of woman he preferred. Having decided to call her in the morning and ask her out, he settled down and went to back to sleep.

He awoke just before seven the next morning. Resisting the urge to call her to interrupt any early lovemaking that might be going on, he called a florist and ordered a dozen roses to be sent to her that afternoon.

"What would you like on the card?"

Good question. "Ah...I want to get to know you. Rick."

* * * * *

I want to get to know you. Jennifer felt a distinct sense of satisfaction as she read the card that accompanied Rick's roses. So he wanted to get to know her, did he? She smiled slowly. Maybe, just maybe she wanted to get to know him too. She tingled as she considered the possibility of taking him on as a casual lover. She remembered the feel of his lips, hands, and cock and bit her bottom lip. Oh, yes, she wanted to get to know him too—at least in a carnal sense. But under no circumstances was she going to allow her heart to become involved. There was no way she was going to allow another blond to hurt her. Love her? Yes and yes again, but no falling in love with another fickle blond.

She had just finished a load of laundry and was trying to decide if she should call Cherica to see how her date of the previous night had gone when her phone rang.

It was Cherica. She put the laundry basket down by the apartment door and snatched up the phone. "Well, it's about time you called!" She grinned. "I guess I don't have to ask what you've been doing."

A short silence ensued. She frowned. "Come on — give."

"Ah, obviously you're expecting someone else. This is Rick."

Her heart thumped. "Oh...hi."

"Hi. Ah...did you get the flowers I sent?"

"Yes." She put a hand over the receiver and took a deep, calming breath. "Red roses. They're beautiful. Thank you."

"Ah...I was wondering if you'd like to have dinner with me some time."

Her cheeks burned as she thought she was more interested in going to bed with him than she was in getting to know him. "Why?"

"Why?" He sound puzzled. "What do you mean why?"

"I mean why. I'll readily admit that I enjoyed our date and what followed, but let's be real, Rick, we're not really suited to each other."

"I disagree. We have shared interests. I think we're very suited to each other, or at least I think there's a good possibility we might be. That's why I want to take you out and get to know you."

"Rick, I'm flattered, but I — "

"Look, I know you say you're not into blonds, but I don't know that I buy that."

"What?"

"I can't imagine that you allow men you're not 'into' to make love to you."

"Are you telling me you think I'm 'into' you?"

"I'm telling you I'd like to get to know you, Jennifer. Nothing more."

Was she interested in actually getting to know him? She suspected that if she invested the time it took to know him, she'd find herself in love with him—alone. She'd been there and done that.

"Jennifer? Can I take you out?"

She wanted to say yes so badly she knew she mustn't. Even knowing that, she had to fight hard to remain silent.

"Jennifer, are you interested? If not, just say so and I won't bother you again."

He sounded annoyed and that rankled. Did he think her size limited her options so that she had to accept every man who asked her out? Well, if he did, it was time he learned better. "I'm not interested," she said and hung up the phone.

Oh, now that was smooth, Jenn and ever so gracious. Mom would be so very proud of you, she told herself angrily. She bit her lip and stood staring at the phone. Maybe he'd realize she hadn't really meant to hang up and call back. "Yeah and maybe you'll be a slender, blonde bombshell when you wake up tomorrow morning."

She gave an angry shake of her. What was done was done. She'd just killed any chance she'd had of forming even a purely physical relationship with him.

Cherica finally called as she was putting away the laundry. "Want to go for a power walk?"

"I'd rather stay home and have a pint or two of ice cream."

Cherica considered in silence for a moment. "What's happened?"

"It's a boring story."

"Come on down. I'll put on some popcorn and we'll talk about it."

"Rica, I am not in a popcorn mood."

"Okay, ice cream it is. Come on down and we'll eat so much ice cream that we'll have to go to the gym and power walk for weeks to get back on scheduled. How's that?"

She smiled. Cherica sounded cheerful and upbeat. Her date with Maurice must have gone very well. "Okay. I'm on my way."

Fifteen minutes later, she and Cherica lay barefoot in twin recliners eating air popcorn and low-fat frozen yogurt. "I was lured here under false pretenses," she grumbled. "I was promised real ice cream and lots of it, too."

Cherica grinned unrepentantly. "Stop your whining and tell me what's wrong."

"Who says anything's wrong?"

"The look of dejection on your face does. So what is it? Is your mom all right?"

She nodded slowly. "Actually, her spirits have been rather high lately." She told Cherica about her mother's new 'friend'.

Cherica widened her eyes. "Wow. Way to go, Mom!"

She frowned. "I'm glad you think it's so wonderful. She's sixty dating a fifty-year old man, for crying out loud. It's a disgrace."

"Really? Have you met him?"

"No."

"Then what are you basing your opinion on?"

"On the age difference! Rica, she's ten years older than him."

"So? If it doesn't bother them why should it bother you?"

"For plenty of reasons. Dad's only been dead ten months and already she's taken up with some young gigolo?"

"Gigolo? I thought you said you hadn't met him."

"I haven't, but Dad hasn't been dead —"

"Jenn, the operative word here is dead. Your dad was a wonderful man, but he's dead and she's alive. She has a right to go on living. Give her a break."

She shook her head. "You don't understand."

"Okay, maybe I don't, but there's something besides your mom's dating bothering you. Is it Blondie?"

She sighed. Cherica's insight never ceased to amaze her. "Okay. I saw him again."

"What? When."

She told her about their brief encounter of the night before and his call earlier that day.

"So why didn't you agree to date him?"

"What would have been the point?"

"Oh, I don't know that there needs to be one beyond the fact that you like him. And don't bother denying that you do like him."

She didn't challenge Cherica's conclusion. They had been best friends too long for that. "I do not intend to have my heart broken by another blond."

Cherica frowned. "How do you know he would break your heart?"

"Because he likes slender blondes."

"Well maybe he also likes full-figured brunettes."

"Not likely."

"Then please explain why he asked you out."

"I don't know, but I know it's not because he likes his women big, otherwise he wouldn't have been with that tiny blonde."

"What tiny blonde?"

"The one from the auction."

"He was with her?"

"Yes and looking at her as if he couldn't wait to get her alone."

"Hmm. Then why did he follow you to the powder room?"

"I...I don't know. Maybe he wants to have his cake and eat it too." She shrugged. "Anyway, I told him I wasn't interested and I don't want to talk about it or him anymore. He's history."

"Ooookay."

She frowned. "I mean it, Rica."

"Okay. You mean it."

"What I really want to talk about is how your date went."

Cherica's pretty face lit up and she smiled. "It went rather well. Actually, it went very well."

"How well?"

"Very well. He asked me out."

"You...you're going out with him again?"

"Yes. Why are you looking at me like that?"

"Like what?"

"Like you're so surprised and shocked."

"Well, I guess I am a little."

"Why?"

"Well, I'm just wondering..." she trailed off. Jayson would be devastated when he found out. "I just didn't expect you two to hit it off."

"Well, he's a nice guy and I think I want to get to know him."

"Did you get to know him last night?"

She shook her head. "No."

"Why not?"

"I thought I'd ask him back to my place, but when it came right down to it...I let him peck me on the cheek and we said goodbye in the lobby. By the time I got up to my apartment, he was on his cell phone, asking me to have dinner with him next week."

"Oh...that's...great."

Cherica sighed. "Go ahead. Say it."

She widened her gaze and feigned surprise. "Say what?"

"Ask me what Jayson will say."

"He's going to be...disappointed."

"If he is, he'll get over it. And really, Jenn, there's no reason for him to care one way or the other."

Boy, was she living in fantasyland.

"Now can we talk about something else?"

Even as she readily nodded, she kept thinking: poor Jayson. He's going to be devastated.

Chapter Six

"You want to talk about it?"

Rick looked across his basement rec room to the other recliner where Troy sat. They were both bushed after playing several sets of tennis. "So now I know why you chose to spend part of your Friday night with me," he said dryly. Although he and Troy were still best friends, these days the only time they spent together outside of work was spent at Troy's house. "You want me to bare my soul...about...?"

Troy shrugged. "I don't know. That's one of the reasons I'm here. To find out."

"And the other reason you're here?"

"Just to spend some time with you. I miss that we don't get to hang out much any more."

"So do I," he admitted.

Troy nodded. "Now that we've gotten the mush out of the way, let's talk about what's been bothering you this last week."

Rick sighed and took a deep sip of his beer. "And if I said nothing's been bothering me?"

"I'd know you were lying. Rick, you've been an absolute menace at work all week, snapping at any and everyone for no reason at all. What happened? Did you two have a fight?"

He sat his beer can in the circular recess in his recliner's arm. "Who are you talking about?"

"You and the blonde. What's her name? Carol?"

"It's Carolyn, but why the hell should you think we'd had a fight? We're not even dating!"

"You're not?" Troy frowned. "Why not?"

"Because I'm not interested in her."

"Since when?"

"Since I took her out and found out what a bitch she is."

Troy raised a brow. "Aaah."

"And what's that supposed to mean?"

"It's your charity date. You had a fight with her?"

"No. We didn't have a fight. She just told me she's not interested in seeing me."

"And you believed her?"

He recalled how firm she'd sounded when she'd said it. And hanging up on him had been pretty decisive too. "Yes. Believe me, she meant what she said."

Troy shrugged. "Fine. She's not the only woman in town. Find another one."

"It's not that simple," he said slowly.

"Why not?"

Because he wanted her. He sighed and shook his head. "I...like her."

"Then ask her out again."

"So she can turn me down again? I think she enjoyed saying no."

"You're not the first man to be turned down by a woman who eventually found that she couldn't live without him after all. Ask her out again or ask someone else out. Do whatever you need to in order to relieve your stress. But do something because everyone at work is afraid of having his or her head taken off if they so much as speak to you."

He frowned. "Have I been that bad?"

"Yes. If you like her that much, ask her out again. Keep asking her out until she accepts."

"Or accuses me of harassing her."

Troy grinned. "Isn't she worth the risk?"

"I...I like her," he said again. But he wasn't sure how much rejection he was prepared to take in the name of "liking" her.

"Did she say why she didn't want to go out with you?"

"She said she wasn't really my type, that she knew I liked slender blondes."

"And so you do."

"Troy, I don't need you telling me kind of women I prefer."

Troy held his hands up, palms outward. "Fine, but if I were you, I wouldn't stress too much over a single refusal."

"She hung up on me."

"So? Maybe she's playing hard to get. Bottom line, Rick, if she spent five hundred dollars to spend a few hours with you, I'll bet she's inclined to like you too. Give it a week or so and call her again. In the meantime, why don't you take some time off?"

"Trying to get me out of the office?"

"Yes. Before all our employees quit."

"Have I been that bad?"

"For the second time, yes."

He laughed. "Okay. I promise to keep my cool and I'll take a day or so off and head down to the shore."

"Good. Now. What did you think about the fight last night?" he asked of a middleweight boxing match between the top contenders.

They discussed sports until Troy left just before eleven. As he lay in bed later, Rick was unsure if he should take Troy's advice and ask Jennifer out again. She'd sounded fairly decisive about not wanting to get to know him. Then he remembered how passionately she had responded to him. Maybe Troy was right. He'd spend a few days down the shore, then he'd come back and ask her out. If she said no again, he'd forget her. Period.

The phone was ringing when Rick got home that night. He put his briefcase on the phone table in the foyer and picked up the cordless phone he kept there. "Hello."

"Hi Rick."

"Carolyn." Just what he needed. "Hi."

"I know I didn't make a good first impression on our first date and I wanted to apologize."

"That's not necessary."

"Yes. It is. I don't want you to think I'm a first class bitch because I'm not."

She'd sure given a good impersonation of one.

"So what I was hoping was that you'd give me a chance to make amends. I was wondering if you'd have lunch with me."

It had taken a certain amount of character, not to mention interest, in him for her to call him like this. He nodded. "I'd like that. When?"

"I'm free tomorrow."

"So am I. Where can I pick you up?"

They arranged to meet at a small restaurant halfway between their respective offices and he hung up. He thought briefly of Jennifer before dismissing her from his thoughts. There were too many available women for him to chase one who didn't want to be caught.

The next afternoon he sat across the table from Carolyn, listening to her talk about her interests, none of which he shared. He knew that no matter how much she liked him, he couldn't get past wishing she liked sports, had dark hair, silver eyes, and a lot more body mass.

She sighed suddenly and looked directly into his eyes. "Anyone home?"

He sat back in his seat. "You're an incredibly beautiful woman, Carolyn."

"And? Go on with the but."

"But we don't really have much in common," he went on.

"Let's go to bed before you decide that," she said.

The offer, which would once had sent his cock jumping to full, rigid attention, barely caused a stir in him. "I'm sure that would be an incredible experience."

She tossed her head and stared at him with a look of agitation in her eyes. "But? What's the but this time, Rick? Have you developed a taste for large, lumpy women?"

The bitch was back. He nodded slowly. "As a matter of fact, I have," he told her coolly. He bit back the urge to add that her nearly flat chest and nonexistent ass left him sexually cold.

She threw her napkin onto the table and stood up. "Fine. Go back to your big, mountain-sized woman."

He watched her walk away. Jennifer wasn't interested in him, but he wasn't about to overcompensate by getting involved with a bitch like Carolyn, even on a temporary basis.

* * * * *

"So who were you with when you ran into Blondie the week before last?"

Jennifer put her last three quarters in the slot machine and watched in resignation as none of the horizontal bars matched. She sighed and turned to look at Cherica, who stood at the slot machine next to her with two buckets filled with nickels.

"What?"

"Who were you with at the club when you ran into Blondie and his blonde?"

She hadn't allowed herself to think much about Rick since she'd hung up on him. Now she frowned as memories of how nice his lips had felt against hers as he'd kissed her breathless, intoxicated her senses. "Jayson."

Cherica paused with her hand raised to push the slot machine play button. "Jayson? Jayson Calihan?"

Jennifer smiled slightly. "I think we've had this conversation before. He's the only Jayson I know, so yes...Jayson Calihan."

Cherica's face lost its color and her lips parted in a wordless 'oh'. "I...I didn't know you and Jayson were...how long have you and Jayson been seeing each other?"

She blinked at Cherica, stunned into speechless.

"Why didn't you tell me you were seeing him?"

"Seeing each other? Rica, Jayson and I are not seeing each other!"

"Oh." Cherica gave her a relieved look. "You ran into each other at the club. Was he...alone?"

Okay. This was going to get a little hairy. "No. Didn't I tell you? He was with me...we were together."

"On a date?"

"Well...sort of."

"You just said you two weren't dating."

"And we're not. He came hoping to take you out. When he learned you were out, he asked me if you were on a date."

Cherica sucked in a breath. "And you told him about Maurice?"

She cast her gaze ceiling-ward. "Of course not. Instead of answering, I suggested he take me out instead and we spent a lovely evening trying not to talk about you." Or at least it had been lovely—until she discovered Rick there with his beautiful blonde. But that was another story.

"Oh...not that Jayson would care, mind you, but I'd just as soon he didn't know I'm seeing Maurice right away."

"Yeah. Dream on, girl."

"You don't believe me," she accused.

"In a word? No."

They exchanged a long silent look. "Okay. Here's the deal. I promise not ask about Blondie if you'll stop trying to make me feel guilty about Jayson. Deal?"

She didn't think she was trying to give her a guilt trip, but she nodded. "Deal." She looked at her empty bucket. "I think I'm going to go for a walk along the boardwalk." She glanced at her watch. Four-thirty. "How about we meet outside of the restaurant on the fourth floor for dinner at six-thirty?"

"Okay, but if you're leaving because you've run out of money, grab a couple of handfuls of mine."

"Thanks, but I don't plan to spend all four days in here." She waved, turned, and walked into Rick.

They stood staring at each other in silence.

"I...sorry," she said finally and darted around him, intent on reaching the nearest exit.

"Jennifer. Wait a minute."

Heart thumping, she turned to face him. "I suppose I owe you an apology for—"

"No. You don't owe me anything." He paused, moistening his lips.

She watched the progression of his tongue moving along his sensual bottom lip. Lord, she'd love to kiss him. And caress him. And fuck him. Have him give her a really hard, pussy-shattering fuck.

"I...I'm...fine. How are you?" She realized that he hadn't asked how she was and felt like an idiot.

"Fair to middling. I was wondering...are you here alone?"

She cast a brief glance at Cherica, who stood just a few feet away, staring at them. "No."

He ran a hand through his hair. "Are you...here with a man?"

"I...actually...no."

He stepped out of the way of a woman struggling with several buckets of coins. "Could I buy you and your friend a drink or maybe dinner?"

"Thanks, but we already have—" she began.

"Yes. Yes, you can. We'd love to have dinner with you. Thank you."

She tore her gaze away from his and saw Cherica, with a bucket in each hand, standing at Rick's side.

Cherica ignored her fierce frown and smiled up at Rick. "You're Rick. I'm Cherica Martin. Jenn and I would love to have dinner with you." She grimaced and glanced down at her buckets. "You know, on second thought, I think I'd better pass. I'm on a winning streak. You two go ahead."

Rick looked at her, a question in his blue-green gaze. "Jennifer? Can I buy you dinner?"

"I...actually, I'm just going to walk along the boardwalk. Then I thought—"

"Rick can go with you and then you two can have dinner later."

"Rica!" she protested.

Cherica gave her a wide-eyed innocent look. "What? Just because I'm on a roll is no reason you and Rick shouldn't go for a walk and have a meal. Go. Enjoy yourselves." She smiled at them both and headed toward the cashier.

He watched Cherica go before turning to look at her again. "I'd really like to buy you dinner, or just walk the boardwalk with you if you'd rather not do dinner."

Oh, who was she kidding? She not only wanted to have dinner with him, she wanted to sleep with him. "I...ah...I'd like that."

He raked a hand through his hair. "Which one? Dinner or the walk?"

"Both," she admitted.

"Both?"

She grinned and shrugged. "I'm the greedy sort. I like my cake and eating it too."

"Is it only cake you'd like to have and eat, Jennifer?"

Looking up into his blue-green eyes, memories of his cock plowing through her pussy assailed her senses. She flushed and looked away. "I think you know that I'm rather fond of...cock."

"Then we're a matched set because I am very, very fond of pussy," he said softly.

She waited in vain for him to personalize it and tell her he was fond of her pussy.

She looked away. "About that walk..."

They walked along the boardwalk. Each time their hands occasionally brushed, she felt a tingle all through her body. Although they talked sports while walking, she kept her gaze straight ahead. Still, she could 'feel' him looking at her.

Midway down the boardwalk he bought her a box of saltwater taffies.

By the time they parted at five-thirty to change for dinner, she had finally admitted to herself that she did want to get to know him.

As they waited for the elevator, she looked up at him. "I'm sorry."

"For what?"

"Hanging up on you."

He shrugged. "Well, it did tend to ruin my entire weekend."

"Did it?"

"Yes."

She moved closer and touched his hand. "If it's any consolation, I regretted it the moment I did it."

He stood aside to allow several people to surge ahead as the elevator doors opened. "You can make it up to me by having dinner with me."

"We're already having dinner."

He put out a hand to stop her as she moved toward the elevator. "Then you can owe me another date."

That wasn't exactly the response for which she'd been hoping. She'd wait for another opportunity and try again later. She nodded. "Okay."

"Okay?" He tilted his head to once side. "Don't you want to torture me with a maybe or we'll see?"

"No." She took a deep breath. "If you want to know the truth…"

"I do…I think. Or at least I want to know it if it's something I'm going to want to hear."

She grimaced. "Now how am I expected to know what you want to hear?"

He put a hand against her back and she stepped through the doors of the elevator that had just opened. To her surprise the doors closed and they had the elevator to themselves. "Oh, I think you know what I want to hear," he told her.

She shrugged. "I was just going to say that I'd like to see you again…that is…if you're still interested."

He brushed the back of his hand against hers, setting her heart to thumping. "I'm still here, aren't I?"

Yeah, but how long would he stay around? What was going to happen once the novelty of dating a full-figured woman wore off?

They parted at her hotel room door, and she took a quick shower and changed into a dark blue dress with a modest neckline and a frilly skirt that fell around her calves.

Cherica came in as she slipped on her heels. "Wow! You look great, Jenn. You'll knock Blondie right off his big feet."

She leered. "Yeah? Well, if he lands on a bed, he'd better watch out. Because I am so damned horny, I'll have him nude and be riding his cock in a New York minute."

Cherica grinned. "There you go. Keep 'em naked, hard, and buried in you to the hilt, I always say."

Her smile vanished. "Might be wishful thinking on my part. He's so much more reserved than he was before. I've been practically throwing myself at him and he hasn't bit yet. I don't think he plans to give me another chance to reject him."

"Do you plan to reject him again?"

"No."

"Then what's the problem? Tell him and clear the air. Just come right out and tell him you want some cock."

She tried to do that several times during dinner, but each time, he just gave a little shake of his head. Finally, she took the hint and started talking sports. After dinner, she took off her stockings and shoes, which he put in his jacket pockets, and they walked along the beach.

They didn't talk at all. As they neared the end of the beach, they encountered a couple sitting on the beach with a small radio playing the Billy Joel song they both liked. Without saying a word, they turned into each other arms and shared a quick but explosive kiss.

"How long are you down here?" he asked when they turned to head back to the other end of the beach and their hotel.

"We're going home Sunday afternoon. You?"

"I'm leaving Monday night."

A lot could happen in the two and a half days before she had to leave. Even if she had to drag him kicking and screaming into bed. She passed her tongue over her lips. She could still almost taste his kiss on her lips. Maybe he'd walk to bed...provided she gave him enough encouragement. "I didn't ask...are *you* here alone?" she asked into the silence.

"Yes."

She turned to face him. "What happened to your blonde beauty?"

"She's not my blonde anything. I took her out one other time after we met you in the club. We had nothing in common and so decided not to see each other again."

"Really? What went wrong?"

He shook his head. "Nothing went wrong. It's not as if we'd been dating and I just stopped seeing her. We just...she's not my type."

"Really? What is your type?"

He shook his head. "I don't know anymore."

She stared up into his blue-green eyes and knew she wanted more than anything to be his type.

"I just know she doesn't interest me anymore. Now, let's talk about your date that night."

She shrugged and began walking again. "What about him?"

He fell into step beside her and reached for her hand. "Is he...are you and he..."

"Are we what?"

"Lovers."

She stopped and blinked at him. "Lovers? Me and...no! He's just a friend."

"He looked at you as if he'd like to be a lot more."

"He did no such thing! We've known each other since high school...as friends."

He gave her hand a squeeze. "You're sure?"

"Yes!"

"And he didn't spend the night with you?"

"No!" She stared at him, feeling her face heat up. Did he think because she had hopped into bed with him after their first date that she was easy?

He sighed. "Wow. That's a relief. I could barely sleep for imagining the two of you spending the night making love."

"Why should that thought bother you?"

"Because I wanted to be with you. You don't know how tempted I was to dump Carolyn and follow you that night from the club."

So her name was Carolyn. And for all her blonde beauty she hadn't been able to keep his interest. Just maybe this Rick Markham really was different from all the other blonds she'd known.

"You know, I called you that night when I got home. When you didn't answer, I was in agony imagining the two of you making love."

"I heard the phone ring, but I was in the tub." She didn't mention that she had been too rattled after having seen him with the blonde Carolyn to remember to take the cordless phone with her into the bathroom.

"Damn, I wished I'd known that. I spent most of the night imagining him kissing, touching, and loving you."

She laughed. "What an imagination. As if he'd want to spend the night with me, even if we weren't just friends."

He stared at her. "What man wouldn't want to spend the night with you?"

"Believe me, I've known lots of such men."

"I mean men with half a brain."

"Not all men like large women," she pointed out, pleased that she didn't feel any bitterness.

"Your size has very little to do with your attraction, Jennifer. You are a beautiful and passionate woman and you would be no matter what size you were."

She smiled up at him, suddenly feeling as if she were the most beautiful woman in the world, or at least on the boardwalk that night.

He returned her smile, his gaze locking with hers. Just looking into his eyes, she felt breathless. He leaned forward and brushed his lips against hers. She leaned into him, linking her arms around his neck.

As they kissed, she felt his cock stirring. She moved one of his hands from her back and settled it on her behind.

Keeping his other arm around her waist, he fondled her rear end while he continued to kiss her. His lips and caresses created a painful, rising need in her. Her pussy ached with need and an insatiable lust for his thick cock.

She was going to have him in her bed and in her cunt that night even if she had to beg for the pleasure. Of course, it would be nice to have him clutch her against him, draw her down to the sand, and fuck the hell out of her. Right there on the beach, but she had no desire to get arrested for fucking in public.

She pressed against his shoulders. After several more quick kisses and a squeeze of her behind, he drew away from her.

She licked her lips. "We...we should go back to the hotel."

He nodded silently.

They covered the rest of the distance to their hotel with their fingers entwined. Jennifer felt like a giddy teenager walking along the boardwalk holding hands with him. She'd learned early that one of the drawbacks to being a plus size gal was the reluctance of her lovers to publicly show signs of affection. In private, all her lovers had displayed a ravenous sexual appetite for her, but none of them had ever kissed her or even held her hand in public as Rick did.

In the lobby of their hotel, waiting for the elevator with a crush of people, he stood close to her, still holding her hand. She looked up at him. "Rick?"

"Yes?"

"Would you like to...can we...I...I need some...some cock tonight," she whispered, her face flushing.

"Some? Are we talking generic cock or do you have a specific cock in mind?"

Her face flamed. "Any cock will do...as long as it's big, hard, thick...and belongs to you. Can we spend the night together?"

She saw a flash of what looked like satisfaction in his eyes as he smiled slowly and nodded. He squeezed her hand and leaned close to whisper against her ear. "You were going to have a hell of a time getting away from me tonight."

"I don't want to get away from you." Not that night or any other night.

"Don't plan on sleeping tonight," he threatened as the elevator doors opened. The hand he used against the small of her back to urge her forward seemed to burn right through her clothes and against her skin.

Inside the elevator, she leaned against his chest. "Sleep isn't what I had in mind for tonight," she confided in a soft voice.

He brushed his lips against her hair and squeezed her hand. "Good, because I don't intend to let you get much."

Chapter Seven

They stopped by the room she was sharing with Cherica so she could leave her a message and pack an overnight bag before getting back on the elevator and going up to his room.

The moment he closed his door, Jennifer's her heart began pounding in her chest and she felt breathless. It seemed such a long time since they had first made love. She turned to look at him. He was a big, handsome man, and a fantastic lover. How had she ever refused a date with him? Granted, she still wasn't sure she could or should trust her heart to him, but she certainly intended to tender a complete and total surrender of her body to him.

He placed her overnight bag near the big bed. "Would you like a drink or anything?"

She shook her head. "At the risk of sound crude, I just want some dick."

"Some dick? Are we talking generic again?"

"Your dick. Satisfied?"

She just wanted to make love.

"No and I won't be until said dick is buried in your very specific pussy."

He took off his jacket and tossed it onto the sofa as he crossed the room to her. He cupped her face between his palms and gently kissed her lips. "Jennifer. Beautiful, sexy, Jennifer. I've been dreaming about you and your pussy since the last time I saw you."

She grinned. "Been longing for some big gal pussy, have you?"

"Shit, yeah. " He gripped her hips and pulled her body tight against his. "As long as you're the big gal the pussy belongs to."

"Hmm. Right answer." She fumbled between their bodies and lowered his zip. "No generic pussy for you, huh?"

"Hell, no," he groaned as she reached into his pants and moved her hand over his cock. "My cock was made just to fit in your sweet, hot pussy, Jennifer."

"You think so, huh?" She nibbled at his lips and closed her fingers over his naked flesh. "You might be right, but just to be on the safe side, I'll have to have a sample. Just to be sure, you understand."

"Oh, baby, I understand perfectly. Just to be on the safe side, I think we'd better fuck all night long."

"Oh, lord, Rick, I want your cock in my pussy."

"It's all yours, Jennifer."

She closed her eyes and allowed her senses to take over. She was so hot, she wouldn't have objected if he'd just ripped their clothes off, pushed her down to the floor, and banged her senseless. Nevertheless, she liked that he took his time. He rained soft yet insistent kisses on her lids, her cheeks, her nose, her throat, and finally on to her waiting lips again. All while she kept her grip on his hot cock.

With a knot of heat and tension coiled in her belly, she began pumping his shaft in his pants.

"Slow down," he moaned "or I'm going to come before I even get my cock out of my pants."

"Oh, no. We can't have that." She carefully drew his shaft out of his pants and reluctantly released her grip on his swelling flesh.

He undressed her leisurely, stopping to kiss and caress with his eyes and hands each part of her body. By the time she stood in front of him in her underwear, the bottom of her panties were already soaked. He removed her bra and spent several mind-numbing minutes kissing and kneading her breasts.

"You are so beautiful...so sweet and sexy. Damn, you make me so hard and horny..."

As she stood trembling and needy, he knelt and removed her panties. Instead of tossing them aside as he'd done with her bra, he held them up to his nose and inhaled slowly and deeply. "Hmm. They smell just like your sweet pussy." He stuffed them in his pants pocket. Still on his knees, he stroked his hands down her inner thighs. Thinking he meant to stroke her mound or finger her to test her readiness for his cock, she parted her legs slightly.

She was stunned when he leaned forward and began planting moist, hungry kisses against her mound and on her pussy. None of her other lovers had ever kissed her pussy. The sensations his mouth aroused in her were incredible. He touched the tip of his tongue to her clit and a bolt of pure lust thundered through her. She moaned, her whole body trembling. "Rick...oh, Rick...please...please."

He licked at her pussy, dipping the tip of his tongue just inside her, at the top of her cunt.

"Hmm."

"Like that, do you, honey?"

"Oooh. Hmm."

He inserted two fingers inside her and fucked them in her while he kissed and nipped at her clit. Her juice flowed over his fingers. Her pussy was on fire for his cock.

"Rick! Please! Please! Give me some cock. Now. My pussy's burning and aching for your cock. Please put it in me."

He planted a final kiss against her mound and rose to his feet. Keeping his gaze locked on hers, he pulled off his clothes. He retrieved several condoms from his pocket, took her hand, and led her to the bed.

She pulled back the covers and climbed onto the bed, lying on her side. He joined her, pressing his body against hers. She could feel his cock, hard and warm against her and a fresh rush of moisture filled her cunt. He tipped up her chin and kissed her. This time his lips against hers were demanding and unyielding. His kisses went on and on until she could barely breathe. She could only respond by clinging helplessly to him while he mounted a relentless assault on her senses.

Tearing his mouth away from hers, he handed her a condom. The thought of holding his dick in her hands as she covered it with a condom added to her rising excitement, and she fumbled with the rubber.

"I'd kind of like to get some pussy sometime tonight," he teased.

She giggled and made only a token protest when he took the rubber from her and rolled it over his shaft. The laughter died when he eased her onto her back and rose over her. She looked down and watched as the head of his cock entered her pussy.

"Oh, God," she moaned. "Don't tease me. Please. Let me have it all. Shove it in. Oh, lord, please shove it deep in me."

"Actually, the name is Rick," he told her and thrust against her until he was balls deep in her.

She closed her eyes and clung to his shoulders, her cunt already convulsing around him. "Oh, God! It's...good...your big cock feels so very good in my cunt. Lord, I love this."

"So do I, baby," he said and pushed his hips forward against hers, driving his cock deep within her, again and again. "You have no idea how good your pussy feels."

She tossed her head back, arching her neck. "Tell. Tell how I feel."

"Sweet, baby. So sweet. You are tight and hot and moist and creamy. Oh, damn, you feel so good." Rotating his hips, he pounded her pussy, digging his cock deep inside her quivering flesh. Wonderful, delicious feeling tore through her, encompassing every particle of her being. The sensations weren't just physical; they touched and ignited her very essence.

She clung to him, shuddering and clutching at his buns. He responded by increasing his pace and thrusts. At the speed he was going, she didn't think either of them would last much longer. The momentum of pleasure was building too fast to go on. Just moments later, thrusting wildly at each other, they both came. She sobbed his name and clung to him. He groaned and collapsed on top of her, burying his face against the side of her neck.

They lay quietly for a time, breathing deeply and holding each other, delighting in the after glow.

She kissed his hair. "You have such soft hair," she told him.

"It's blond," he murmured. "You don't like guys with blond hair."

"Don't I?" She opened her eyes and realized for the first time that they'd made love with the lights on, something she hadn't done since her freshman year of college. His hair gleamed in the light from the bedside lamps. "I can't imagine you with any other color hair."

He lifted his head and looked down at her. "Is that a compliment, Jennifer?"

"It's a statement," she countered. "We…ah…we should turn the lights out."

"Why?" He raised his upper body from hers and looked down at her breasts.

They were big and they sagged something awful the moment she took off her bra. She didn't want him staring at them. "I'm not used to making love with the lights on."

"We've already made love with them on, Jennifer." He bent and suckled at her breasts. He murmured something she didn't quite catch.

"What?" She gasped the word. His mouth and tongue on her breasts were creating a new level of need in her.

He rolled off of her and she watched, her face burning, as he discarded the condom and put on another one. "I said we've already made love with them on and we are about to do it again. Unless, of course, you object."

If he didn't, why should she? She shook her head.

Their lovemaking the second time was much more leisurely and even more devastating. He overwhelmed her. He brushed his lips against her closed eyelids and her nose. He kissed her cheeks. He blew in her ears, nipped her lobes, and caressed her breasts. He did something no other man had ever done. He moistened his finger in her pussy and then gently probed her ass.

Instead of pain, after the first wave of shock, she felt a pleasing jolt.

"Do you like that?" he asked, his little finger buried in her virgin ass to the first joint.

"It feels...nice," she admitted, in a shamed voice. "But I...I don't do...I've never...your cock is too big to go up my ass."

He laughed softly and gently withdrew his finger. "Don't worry, Jennifer. It's your pussy that totally enchants me, not your ass. Lovely though it is. Now that's not to say that one of these days I wouldn't like a piece of your sweet ass."

"Maybe, but don't count on putting your big hot sausage up there."

"Don't you like hot sausages?"

"I love them — in my pussy."

He rolled off of her and gently thumbed her clit before inserting his middle finger inside her. He started countless sensual fires burning in her. Her entire body was consumed with heat and pleasure as he made love to her. His hands and lips touched all of her hot spots and created new ones — everywhere he touched.

"You are so beautiful, Jennifer...I love making love to you...being inside you gives me a level of pleasure and contentment I've never felt with any other woman...you rock my world, baby."

Listening to his passionate declarations as he made love to her, she felt beautiful, desirable, and capable of fulfilling all his sexual needs and fantasies.

He had a way of rotating his hips and then thrusting his cock deep within her with so much power and passion that her toes curled. Her whole body melted with longing and need. They made love again and finally fell asleep in the early morning.

* * * * *

Several hours later, Jennifer woke alone in bed. She lay with her face pressed against the pillow, slowly inhaling the faint scent of Rick's cologne that lingered there before she opened her eyes.

From the bed, she had a perfect view of the ocean. Smiling, she turned her head and saw Rick, wearing a pair of briefs, sitting in a chair in front of the window looking out at the ocean.

She looked around for her clothes and saw them across the big room, on the sofa. She grimaced. He would put them in a place that required her to walk naked in front of him to retrieve them. She smiled when she noticed the robe tossed across the foot of the bed.

It seemed she'd maligned him. She got up and slipped it on. He turned his head and smiled at her. "Hi."

"Hi."

"Are you hungry?"

She nodded.

"I ordered room service. I wasn't sure when you'd wake up, so it won't be here for another half an hour or so."

"Okay. That'll give me time to shower and dress."

"Before you do that..." He extended a hand.

She shook her head. "What? You want something?"

"Yes. You."

She blinked at him. "Me?"

"Yes. Come here."

Tightening the robe around her body she walked across the room to the chair and placed her hand in his. He tugged on it and she realized he wanted her to sit on his lap.

She stared down at him. "Are you sure? I've never met a man who wanted me to sit on his...hey!"

He tugged her off balance and she fell onto his lap. He immediately wrapped his arms around her and pressed his lips against her neck. "Well, now you have."

She shifted her body and turned to look at him. "I...I should go shower and dress."

"In a few moments," he said and pressed his cheek against hers. "I just want to hold you for awhile. Is that too much to ask?"

"No." The single syllable was all she could manage past the sudden lump in her throat.

He brushed his lips against hers and slipped his hand inside the robe to fondle her breasts.

"Oh, that feels so good," she whispered and turned her head, in search of his lips.

"God, I love your tits," he told her.

She'd never particularly liked having her breasts referred to as knockers or tits or any of the other slang terms men used, but hearing him talk about how much he liked her tits excited her.

"They sag."

He lifted his head with a surprised look on his handsome face. "Do they? Do they really? Well, I have news for you, honey. I love big tits that sag."

"Really?"

"Oh, yeah, baby." He leered at her. "Such large tits to suck and so little time. What's a poor boy to do?"

"Suck harder and faster."

They spent several minutes kissing and cuddling. With his hands moving from her breasts to stroke over her stomach and thighs, it didn't take long before she was damp between her legs and longing to feel his cock sliding into her pussy again.

Finally, as she was about to suggest they go back to bed, he lifted his lips from hers. "Damn. I almost forget. Your friend called while you were asleep."

"Cherica?" She drew back so she could see his face. "How did she sound? Was everything okay?"

"I guess. She wanted you to call her when you woke."

"Oh." She gave him a quick kiss and stood up. She called their hotel room, but received no answer. She glanced at Rick's watch, which lay on the table by the phone. It was nearly eleven o'clock. Cherica wasn't likely to still be asleep. She hung up and dialed Cherica's cell phone.

She answered on the third ring. "Hello?"

"Rica? Where are you? Is everything all right?"

"Everything's fine. What about you? How are you feeling?"

"Fine...actually...great."

"You enjoyed last night?"

"Yes."

"Good. Looking forward to spending more time with Blondie?"

"Yes."

"Good. Then I did the right thing."

She knew that tone of voice. "What right thing did you do?"

"Two's company, Jenn, three's a crowd. I know the two of you need time alone together if you're going to get your relationship off the ground. And I know that's what you want, even if you won't admit it."

"Rica, what have you done?"

"Nothing much. I just packed both of our bags, dropped yours off at the reception desk, gave up our room, and am just fifteen minutes away from home. You can thank me later."

"Thank you later?! Rica, are you crazy? What possessed you? How could you do this?"

"It needed to be done. I know you're angry now, but—"

"Angry?! Rica, you have no idea. When I get my hands on you—"

"We'll discuss it later. Give Blondie a big, juicy kiss for me. See you in a few days. Bye."

She slammed the phone down on its cradle.

Rick rose and put a hand on her waist. "Jennifer? Is everything okay?"

She turned to face him. "I don't believe her."

"What happened?"

"We came here in her car. She...she gave up our room, dumped my suitcase at the reception desk, and now she's nearly home. She stranded me here!"

"Why would she do that?"

She willed herself not to blush. "You saw how she threw us at each other last night. You can imagine why she did it."

"Then let's not disappoint her." He brushed the back of his hand against her cheek. "I would love to have you stay here with me. I'll drive you home Sunday."

"You weren't planning to leave until Monday."

He shrugged. "I'll leave with you on Sunday. It was going to be pretty dull down here once you left anyway. So will you stay or shall I drive you home today?"

She shook her head and burrowed against him. "I'll stay."

He hugged her. "Well, if you're going to be that easy to get along with, why don't we stay until Monday?"

She smiled up at him. "You know what? I would love to stay here with you until Monday."

"This calls for a celebration." He grinned and pushed the robe off her shoulders. "Let's go make love."

"What about room service?"

"They can leave it outside the door or take it back. We'll order something else later." He slipped his arms around her and stroked his hands down her behind. "Right now my appetite is not for food. I want to take you to bed and do all kinds of wicked things to you."

She smiled and ground her body against his thickening shaft. "Really? Like what?"

"Like suck your breasts and pussy, and lick your sweet cheeks while I finger fuck your ass."

"I'm rather fond of big, handsome, blond men who want to do wicked things to me."

"Yeah? Then I'm your man."

He was definitely going to be her man for the next few days. After that? Well, she wasn't going to think about anything beyond Monday.

He put out the do not disturb sign on the door handle and they went back to bed. They made love twice before cuddling. "Are you going to let me fuck your ass?" he murmured as she teetered on the edge of sleep.

"You are a greedy so and so," she complained, holding him close. "You pounded my pussy unmercifully, now you want to do the same to my ass."

"I'll be gentle," he promised.

"I'll think about it, but it'll be a big step for me, Rick."

"Then we'll wait until you're ready for it." He kissed her hair. "Don't worry about it. One day you'll want to try it. When you do, I'll be ready."

* * * * *

During the next two and a half days, Rick found himself totally enchanted with Jennifer. In addition to being one of the loveliest women he'd ever met, she was also passionate and refreshingly frank about being sexually attracted to him. And he'd finger fucked her ass several times since the first time and every time he knew she enjoyed it more.

Still, he knew she wasn't going to let him fuck her ass. To his surprise, he was okay with that. Her pussy was more than enough to keep his cock hard and his interest in her high.

As an added bonus, she could and did talk sports with enthusiasm and intelligence. Damn. What a lovely, enthralling woman.

By the time they left the hotel on Monday morning, he knew he wanted a serious relationship with her. He wasn't quite ready to acknowledge that he was falling for her or that he could envision marrying her. Even so, he knew he wanted to lay a big enough claim on her affection and attention so that she didn't want to see any other man while they explored their chances of becoming a permanent couple and maybe more.

Her willing response to his lovemaking notwithstanding, his certainty that her feelings about blond men hadn't really changed kept him silent. When he left her at her apartment that afternoon, he found it difficult not to tell her he wanted to see her exclusively.

He contented himself with kissing her slowly while he finger fucked her bottom. The fact that they were both dressed, enhanced the experience for him. Of course she wasn't wearing any underwear. Come to that, neither was he. They had spent the entire drive with his zip down and his cock outside his pants and the front of her skirt pushed up to her waist.

They had fingered and fondled each other for most of the way. Remembering, he smiled. It was a good thing he had leather seats because they had both come.

They were now up to two fingers in her ass. She whimpered and he felt her rectal muscles tightening against his fingers. He gripped her hip with his free hand and slammed his fingers in and out of her clinging hole.

She gasped and dropped her head against his shoulder. "Oh, Rick! I never knew having something in my bottom could feel so good."

He smiled and gently withdrew his fingers. "Your ass, Jenn, like the rest of your body, is totally delicious and intoxicating. And you are going to let me fuck your ass one of these days."

"Maybe."

He smiled her. "I have to go. I'll call you."

She nodded, not quite meeting his gaze. "Sure."

He tipped up her chin so he could look down into her beautiful silver-gray eyes. "I will call you, Jennifer."

"I know. I just…"

"What?"

She linked her arms around his neck and brushed her lips against his, making his cock stir. "Nothing. I just need a little time. Okay?"

"A little time for what?"

"To decide if you're for real."

"I am."

"I need to reach that conclusion on my own."

It amazed him that she hadn't determined that already. He felt so raw, as if his feelings were on display for everyone to see. After all, Troy had readily seen how stressed he was. But then, Troy was his best friend. Clearly, she was going to need time to realize how he felt.

"Can you handle that, Rick?"

"I'll have to, won't I?" He bent and kissed her again. "I'll talk to you soon."

She stroked her fingers through the hair at the back of his neck. "Okay."

He headed straight for work after leaving her. After checking with the secretary he and Troy shared to make sure there was nothing pressing awaiting his attention, he made his way to Troy's office.

Troy looked up at his knock and waved him in. "Ah, the prodigal returns. Sit."

Instead of sitting in one of the chairs in front of Troy's desk, he stretched out on the leather sofa along one wall and closed his eyes.

"Okay. You look well rested, but clearly you've been doing something over the weekend other than sleeping."

Neither he nor Jennifer had had much sleep during the past three and a half days, not that he was about to admit that to Troy. "Bev tells me we've finally heard back from Wilco Gaming."

"Ah, so we don't want to talk about the long weekend?"

"No we don't," he said, smiling slightly. "Let's talk about Wilco Gaming."

"In a moment. Are you feeling better?"

"Yes," he admitted, although he wasn't quite sure why. His gut instinct told him he was going to have to work to convince Jennifer that he could be trusted.

"Then I assume you decided to give Carolyn another chance."

He bolted into a sitting position and stared at Troy. "You assume wrong. I have no interest in her. None. Zero. Squat. Understood?"

Troy nodded. "I think you've made your lack of interest in her crystal clear. So then...you've seen Jennifer over the weekend."

What was the use in denying it? He and Troy knew each other too well for either one of them to be able to deceive the other for long. "Yes." He closed his eyes and lay back against the sofa.

"That explains the lessening of tension in you."

He sighed, opened his eyes, and turned to look at Troy. "Lessening of tension?"

"Yes. Last week you were wound so tight, it's a wonder you didn't implode. I still sense some tension in you, which makes me believe that things didn't go quite as well with her as you'd have liked. You want to talk about it?"

Sometimes best friends were a damned pain in the ass. "No."

Troy leaned back in his chair. "What seems to be the source of problems between you two?"

"She's been hurt before," he said slowly.

"And how is that your fault or problem?"

"From what I can surmise, the culprit or culprits, I'm not sure which, were blond. She doesn't trust men with blond hair."

An incredulous look passed over Troy's face. "The hell you say."

"No. The hell with men with blond hair she says."

"That rather puts you in a bind with your blond mop top, doesn't it? Of course, there are plenty of women who have a thing for guys with blond hair. You could go find a couple of them."

He closed his eyes and crossed his arms. "I'm getting too old to want more than one woman at a time. I want to settle down with one woman and start a family."

"Ah. In love with her, are you?"

"I like her...a lot."

"That's what I thought...you're in love with her."

"I didn't say that, Troy," he protested.

"But you are, whether you say it or not."

"I like her. That's my story and I'm sticking to it."

Troy laughed. "Go ahead. See if it does you any more good than my refusal to admit I was in love with Angie until you started taking her out."

He bolted into a sitting position and leveled a finger at Troy. "You're not going to ask her out, are you?"

"What?! Now I know you're in love because you're talking like a complete lunatic. Why the hell would I want to take your woman out? Aside from the fact that I'm very, very happily married, she's not my type."

"Not your type? Since when don't you go for beautiful, full-figured women?"

"I've never gone for them," Troy said, surprising him. "Rick, I don't love Angie because she's full-figured. I love her because she's Angie. I realized that when I started dating other full-figured women after she dumped me on the cruise and none of them turned me on. Although I'm crazy in love with Angie and probably always will be, I don't know that my preference in women has necessarily changed."

"Well, mine has," he said. "After Jennifer, I can never imagine getting a hard on over a skinny, flat-chested blonde with no ass again."

"Skinny, flat-chested blonde with no ass, huh? Wow! We are in love, big-time."

He shook his head. "Stop putting words in my mouth, Troy. I like her. Period."

"Is that why you looked like you were ready to come off that sofa and punch me out when you thought I might pull one of your stunts and ask her out to make you jealous?"

He grimaced. "That was different. You and Angie were so clearly right for each other. I wasn't going to let you risk letting her get away because you wouldn't admit the obvious. As your best friend, it was my job to do everything I could to prevent that from happening."

"Never let it be said that I'm not your best friend." Troy arched a brow. "What can I do? My hands are tied. I'll just have to bit the bullet and ask her out."

They stared at each other in silence. The muscles in Troy's face twitched first and then they both laughed.

When they sobered he asked about Wilco Gaming.

Troy sighed. "We have a lot of competition, Rick. We're going to have to work hard and do a lot of wining and dining to land that account."

He shrugged. "We'll get it," he said. If they were successful in landing Wilco Gaming for a client, it would significantly improve their bottom line. "I'll get right on it. What's their rep's name?"

"Connie Betton. We had lunch Friday. Although she was impressed that we're a civic-minded firm, I can tell you she's going to be a tough sell. You'll need all that fabled Markham charm to land this account."

He grinned at Troy. "You concentrate on the design phase and leave the wining and dining to me."

"I thought you'd say that. So I took the liberty of setting up a dinner appointment for the two of you for tomorrow night at The Garden Room."

He frowned. Great. He'd half planned to ask Jennifer to have dinner with him.

"Problem?"

He shook his head. He'd have dinner with this Connie Betton on Tuesday. Although he wanted to see her, Jennifer had said she needed time. He'd wait a week or so, then he'll call her and see if she'd like to have dinner or go to a ballgame with him. "No. I can handle dinner with her tomorrow night."

Chapter Eight

"Are you still angry?"

Jennifer tossed the sketch she'd been attempting to make of Rick aside and stared at Cherica, who stood in front of her balcony doors. "The next time we go anywhere together, I'm taking my car. If I should just happen to leave the room, I'm taking my car keys with me. You won't ever get another chance to go off and leave me stranded in another state again."

Cherica rolled her eyes. "Oh, don't be so dramatic, Jenn. You know perfectly well that I wouldn't have left if I'd really thought you were going to be stranded."

"How did you know I wouldn't be?"

"Are you kidding or are you just blind? Couldn't you see the way he looked at you when you ran into him in the casino? I knew there was no way that man wouldn't have taken you anywhere you wanted to go. And don't bother pretending you didn't have an absolutely fabulous time with him."

She was angry. She'd been spoiling for a fight with someone...anyone since Monday afternoon when Rick had left her at her apartment door with a promise to call her soon. It was now Wednesday night and although he had sent her a dozen red roses Monday, she was still waiting for him to call. Taking her frustration out on Cherica wouldn't accomplish anything. Besides, Cherica was right. Had she stayed around, she and Rick wouldn't have spent nearly as much time together has they had.

"Admit it, Jenn. You had a good time."

She raked a hand through her hair. "Oh, all right. I had a very good time." She smiled. "Oh, Rica. He is so romantic. We walked along the boardwalk and on the beach holding hands. He loves me to sit on his lap to cuddle. He acted as if he couldn't get enough of me. All the things I consider blemishes in myself, he loves. He actually likes my big ass. He couldn't keep his hands off it, or his mouth off my breasts, or his fingers out of my pussy."

Cherica leered at her. "I'm betting his fingers weren't the only thing he couldn't keep out of there."

She blushed. "He's...oh, man is he a great lover."

"Nicely equipped, is he?"

"Very nicely equipped and he...yes."

"So when are you seeing him again?"

She shrugged. "I don't know. He said he'd call."

"When?"

"Monday."

"You mean he hasn't called since you got back?"

"No. He sent roses, but...he hasn't called yet."

"So that's why you're so snappy."

"I am not snappy!"

Cherica tilted her head to one side. "You know, Jenn, you could call him."

"I know."

"But?"

"But I want him to call me."

"I'm sure he will, but Jenn, you know men. Sometimes you have to give them a shove or two in the right direction. If you want to hear from him before he gets around to calling you, call him."

She shook her head. She wasn't going to go chasing after another blond, who'd probably only end up hurting her. "Never mind Blondie. What's going on with you and Maurice?"

Cherica glanced away. "He's...he's a nice guy and before you ask, he's an adequate lover."

"Only adequate?"

She shrugged. "Hey, it happens. Every man can't be as nicely equipped as your big blond."

"Oh. So, he...he's..."

"He's average, but you know what they say."

"About size not mattering?"

Cherica nodded.

"Really? Well, I hate to disagree with 'they', but I happen to think there are few things in the world one quarter as wonderful as a handsome man wielding a big cock he knows who to use."

Cherica sighed. "Well, it doesn't have to be big, but it would help if it was at least thick or something...just so you'd know you were being made love to."

"That bad, huh?"

"He's a nice guy."

She nodded, wondering if Maurice was really as ill-equipped as Cherica said or if her dissatisfaction with him as a lover stemmed from her unacknowledged feelings for Jayson. She knew, however, better than to suggest that. "So are you going to go on seeing him?"

"I guess...like I said, he's a nice guy."

So was Jayson, but she knew better than to mention that too.

* * * * *

Jennifer slept badly that night and awoke feeling irritable and cranky. The day didn't get any better when she spent an entire morning in front of her computer, staring at a blank white screen. She had a deadline looming, but all her characters seemed as cranky as she and refused to cooperate.

Feeling in need of a break, she decided to treat herself to lunch. She chose a quiet café in the mall several miles from her apartment complex. She resisted the urge to have a few drinks before heading home, where she spent the rest of the afternoon in front of a new blank white screen.

She had a sandwich for dinner, lay feeling sorry for herself in a bubble bath for over an hour before drying off and getting into bed. She was rereading the first page of her favorite sci-fi author for the third time when her phone rang. She tossed the book onto the bed and picked up the phone. "Hello?"

"Hi."

Finally. She closed her eyes and leaned back against the pillows propped against her back. "Rick. Hi."

"I know it's late, but I wanted to talk to you. Were you asleep?"

"No. Just reading."

"Did you watch the game?"

She shook her head. Instead of watching the baseball game, she'd sat staring at yet another blank white screen. "No. So. How was your day?"

"Long and frustrating." He went on to tell her of all the problems he'd had that day. He broke off abruptly. "I didn't call to bore you with dreary details of my lousy day. How was your day?"

"Almost as frustrating as yours sounds. None of my characters would cooperate. I have everything I wanted to say and have happen neatly plotted out in my head, but I couldn't seem to transfer it from my head to my computer."

"You never told me what it is you write."

"Oh. Well, probably nothing you've read."

"Try me. What exactly do you write? If it's not something I read, I may develop an appetite for it...just as I've developed one for you."

A wide smile spread across her face. "I...write erotica."

"Erotica? Porn?"

"No! Not porn. There's a difference between the two."

"Okay. There's a difference."

"A big one, Rick."

"Okay. What exactly is the big difference?"

"If you have to ask —"

"Never mind," he said, cutting her off. "Where can I buy some of your...books, are they?"

"Yes."

"Do you write under your own name?"

"No."

"What's your pen name?"

"Rick, I appreciate your interest, but I'm sure you wouldn't like what I write."

"Tell me and let me be the judge. What name do you write under?

"Actually, I had two pseudonyms."

"And they are?"

"I write erotic romances as Desiree Ladu."

"Spell that."

She did.

"And your other pen name?"

"I write erotic thrillers under the pseudonym of D J Savage."

"What? Did you say D J Savage?"

"Yes...why? Have you heard of me?"

"I've done more than heard of you. I'm a fan. I have been since I read Night Desires."

Night Desires, the fourth in a six book series had been written three years earlier and had been so successful she had taken the plunge and began writing full time. "Really?"

"I can't believe you're D J Savage. I thought you were a man."

"Sorry to disappoint," she teased.

"Who the hell said anything about being disappointed? You know damn well I'm very glad you're not a man, Jennifer."

"When we're together, I'm rather glad of that too," she said.

"So...when is your next book coming out?"

"I don't know...weren't you listening when I told you none of my characters would cooperate?" she snapped, annoyed that he'd chosen to ignore her come-on.

"You sound tired and actually, so I am. I'll let you go so you can get some sleep. Good night, Jennifer."

"Ah...yeah...good night." She sighed and hung up. Disappointment rose like bile in her throat. She'd spent the last three days waiting for him to call and now that he had, he hung up without asking her out or even saying he'll call her again. Worse, she'd wasted an entire day, unable to write because he hadn't called. This was not going to work. She was going to have to put some distance between them or risk having her heart broken again.

The next time he got around to calling her, she was going to be too busy to talk to him. She was not going to get hurt again.

The ringing phone startled her. Frowning, she picked it up again. "Hello?"

"Hi. Me again. Damn, I forgot to ask if you'd like to go to the businessman special with me tomorrow afternoon? I know you have a deadline, but I really would like to see you."

"I'd like to see you too," she said. "Yes."

"Great. I have a lunch meeting that will make time kind of tight for me. Would it be too much to ask you to take the subway to the stadium and meet me in front of the baseball stadium at two-thirty?"

"No problem, but I'll drive."

"Take the sub. Please."

"Why?"

"Because if you take your car too, we'll have to come back in separate cars and I want to drive you back."

She felt a foolish smile spreading across her face. "Okay."

"Okay?"

"Yes."

"Good. Jennifer, remember no panties. I want full access to your pussy at the stadium and on the way home."

"If you think I'm going to let you finger me in public, you're playing with a very loose deck."

"Leave your panties home."

"I'll think about it."

"If you wear them, I'll just be forced to take them off and add them to my collection."

"Oh, no you won't," she said quickly. Over the long weekend, he'd pocketed four pair of her panties, which he had not returned.

"Then leave them home. Jenn?"

"Yes?"

"I'm really looking forward to seeing you tomorrow."

The smile turned into a wide grin. "I'll see you then."

"Good night."

"Good night."

Still smiling, she turned off the light and lay down. She'd play hard to get another time...maybe.

* * * * *

Rick found it difficult to concentrate on his lunch with Connie Betton. He was eager to see Jennifer and the meeting seemed to drag on and on. She ate slowly and refused to discuss anything even remotely related to business until she'd eaten. Since he felt as if nothing was being accomplished, he was hard pressed not to cut their meeting short and ask Jennifer to meet him early.

"Well, this has been very enlightening, Mr. Markham. I will certainly consider your proposal," she said as they parted company outside the restaurant. "After you've revised your specs. When do you think you can have revised specs for review?"

"I'm not sure," he admitted. Troy and the design team had been burning the midnight oil for two weeks to come up with the current specs which she was now saying weren't up to par. "I'll be in touch."

"Fine. When you're ready with the revisions, call my secretary and we'll set up a dinner meeting."

Great. Just what he wanted — to suffer through another meal with her. "I'll do that. I'll be in touch."

He ran into a traffic jam and arrived at the stadium fifteen minutes after the game had began. He found Jennifer waiting outside gate G. She had her long, dark hair in a casual ponytail and very little makeup. She looked good enough to eat.

"I was beginning to think I'd been stood up."

"Never." He bent to kiss her. As he did, he drew her close and slipped down the zipper of her slacks.

"Rick!" she hissed his name. "What are you doing?"

"Checking to make sure you are not overdressed."

His probing finger found her pussy bare and warm. He dipped a finger inside her and rotated it. Damn, this woman excited him. He gave her a quick kiss and withdrew his finger.

With her face flushing, she quickly zipped her pants.

He watched, smiling and suggestively licking the finger he had removed from her. "Hmm. Tasty."

"You are an uncultured brute," she told him, lifting her chin.

"Me?" he arched a brow. "I'm not the one without panties."

Her face flamed and just for a moment, he thought she would slap him. "You're uncultured and late."

He grinned unrepentantly. "I know. I'm sorry. The meeting ran longer than I expected and then I hit a traffic jam. Forgive me?"

She smiled suddenly, her beautiful eyes gleaming, and he longed to forget the game and take her home to bed. "We're missing the game," she reminded him.

They had seats under the overhang. Although the day was warm, it was cold in their section of the stadium. He'd brought a small blanket, which he tossed across their mid sections. Under cover of the blanket, he unzipped his pants and slipped his cock out. Without taking his eyes off the action on the field, he reached for her hand, and placed it on his cock.

Although she sucked in a breath, he was pleased that she immediately began fondling his cock. He returned the favor by undoing her zip and slipping two fingers into her pussy.

With fans screaming and cheering around them, they gently fondled and fingered each other until they both came. At least, he thought she came. Her pussy contracted around his fingers, her ass jumped in the seat, and she let out a small gasp, which she stifled by biting the side of one hand.

As for him, he got off on knowing they were almost having sex in a stadium full of people. His cum shot out of his cock head and onto the hand tenderly pumping him. Breathing deeply, he withdrew his drenched fingers from her pussy and uncaring who might be watching, he licked them clean.

She withdrew her hand from his cock. He felt her wiping it on the inside of the blanket.

He slid up his zip. "Was that as good for you as it was for me?" he asked softly, leaning close to her.

"No," she said shortly, her face flushing.

"Liar," he accused.

She looked at him with more than a hint of desire in her silver eyes. "You just keep your big, hot hand to yourself and your dick in your pants, buster."

He laughed and kissed her cheek.

As he looked away from her, he noticed an older man with gray, thinning hair sitting several rows below looking up at them. The man glanced at Jennifer before giving him a knowing grin. He realized that the man had known exactly what had just happened between him and Jennifer.

He shrugged and looked at Jennifer. Her gaze and attention was now focused strictly on the game. She shouted suddenly and along with most of the fans, shot to her feet as the home team third basemen slid into home a breath ahead of the opposing team pitcher's tag.

Two hours later, nearly hoarse from screaming their team to victory, they emerged from the stadium. He couldn't remember the last time he'd enjoyed a game so much. "That was fun," he said. He held her hand as they walked to the parking lot.

"What? The game or the seat sex?" she asked.

"Both." He hesitated. "Did you object? I mean…did you want me to stop?"

She gave him one of those smiles that so enchanted him — one part shy, one part I-am-all-woman-and-I-can-and-will-rock-your-world bold. "Did my pussy feel like I wanted you to stop?"

"No."

"One thing, Rick. Just don't think every time we go to a game I'm going to let you finger fuck me or jerk you off. Because it ain't gonna happen, buster."

He thought of the man back at the stadium and nodded slowly. He didn't want to subject her to the stares and leers of other men who might think her cheap or easy. "Understood. What does your schedule look like?" he asked, as he pulled out of the stadium parking lot. "Did you get any writing done today?"

"Yes. I got up early and wrote for several hours before I left home. So I'm nearly back on schedule."

"Great. Can you play hooky for the rest of the day?"

"That depends."

"On what?"

"On what you have in mind. What else?"

"I thought we could have an early dinner and then I thought...I hoped...would you like to come to my house for a while?"

"A while?"

"Okay. For the night."

"You want me to spend the night at your house?"

"If you'd rather not, we can spend the night at your place."

Traffic ahead was moving quickly so he had to keep his gaze on the road. She was silent for several moments and he wondered if she resented his assuming they would spend the night together. He was trying to decide if he should apologize when she placed a hand on his thigh. "Your house is fine, but we'll need to stop at my place for an overnight bag first."

Instead of going out, he decided to cook for her. Dinner, although simple, took a long time to prepare. She insisted on "helping" him and they spent as much time kissing and caressing as they did peeling potatoes and grilling the steaks and vegetables.

"There," she said, putting their plates on the table on the terrace. "We're ready to eat."

He put his arms around her and pressed his face against the back of her neck. "I'd rather eat you."

She laughed and turned in his arms, linking her arms around his neck. "I think I'd like that, but if you're going to keep me up half the night, the least you can do is feed me first. Food now and other things later."

He reluctantly released her and they sat down. While they rehashed the ballgame during dinner, he kept thinking how beautiful she was and how right having her there felt.

"If you keep staring at me like that, you're going to give me a complex," she warned as they cleared the table.

He smiled and followed her inside. After putting the dishes in the dishwasher, they went back to the rec room. He turned on the stereo, sat in his favorite chair, and urged her down onto his lap.

"You smell good," he told her, burying his face in her hair. He ran his hands over her breasts. "You feel good. Oh, damn, I want you."

"I want you too," she whispered, arching her neck.

"I can't wait to undress you and kiss your beautiful breasts and fondle your behind. Let's go to bed." He kissed her and unbuttoned her blouse.

"Yes," she whispered and rose.

They were halfway across the rec room when his doorbell rang. He glanced at his watch. It was just after eight-thirty, but he wasn't expecting anyone. He went over to the intercom button near the door of the rec room. "Yes?"

"Richard, dear?"

He released the intercom button. "Oh, no," he said softly.

She looked up at him. "Rick? What's wrong?"

"Button your blouse and comb your hair." He reached in his pocket and handed her his comb. "It's my mother."

"Your...mother?"

She sound so surprised, he smiled. "Yes. I do have one, you know." He pushed the intercom button again. "Mom, I'm coming." He looked at her and shrugged. "Come meet my mom."

"Maybe I should wait down here and—"

"No. You're not hiding down here. Button up and follow me upstairs when you're ready." He kissed her quickly and ran up the stairs to admit his mother.

He kissed her cheek and gave her a brief hug. "This is a surprise, Mom."

"A pleasant one I hope, dear." She breezed pass him into the foyer. She stopped abruptly and he turned to see Jennifer disappear into the living room.

She looked at him. "You have company? Have I come at a bad time?"

"Of course not," he lied.

"I can't help feeling that I'm interrupting."

"You're not."

"Well, then I guess you always wear lipstick these days, Richard dear."

He wiped his mouth with the back of one hand and followed his mother into the living room.

"Mom, this is Jennifer Rose. Jennifer, this is my mother, Serena Markham.

He watched his mother size up Jennifer as they shook hands.

"Would you like something to drink, Mom?"

"No, dear." She smiled briefly at him and turned to look at Jennifer, who sat across from her on the sofa. "Jennifer. What a lovely name."

"Thank you."

"And your plans for the future? What are they, dear?"

"My plans? I'm not sure I follow you."

"Exactly how old are you, Jennifer?"

"Twenty-nine, Mrs. Markham."

"Are you married, dear?"

"Married? No."

"But you would like to get married one day?"

"Yes…of course."

"And have children?"

"Ah…yes."

"Of course."

Rick sighed. Jennifer, while looking as if she'd been run over by a steamroller, answered the questions fired at her in a quiet, but firm voice.

His mother looked at Jennifer with an unblinking stare for an embarrassing length of time before looking at him. "Richard, may I speak to you?"

"Of course."

She glanced at Jennifer again. "No. I mean in private."

Jennifer blanched and he gritted his teeth, angered and dismayed by his mother's uncharacteristic lack of grace. Clearly, she didn't approve of Jennifer and didn't mind letting her know it.

He shook his head. "We can talk later, Mom."

"I'd really like to talk to you now, Richard."

"Mother—"

"It won't take long and I'm sure Jennifer will excuse us. Do you mind, Jennifer?"

With her whole face like an expressionless mask, Jennifer shook her head and looked away.

He sighed. He had hoped that when and if they ever met, Jennifer and his mother would like each other. That was now out of the question. There was no way his mother would behave so badly if she approved of Jennifer. Hell, she'd never behaved this way no matter how much she disapproved of the women he'd introduced her to.

Holding onto his temper with difficulty, he followed his mother into the kitchen.

She spun around and stared up at him, her eyes wide. "Where in the world did you meet her?"

"What do you mean where did I meet her?" he asked defensively.

"Well, Richard, you have to admit that she's much different from the usual women you bring home."

He resisted pointing out that she had come unannounced and in this instance, was totally unwelcome. "Look, Mom, I know she's nothing like the women I'm usually attracted to, but I didn't think you'd be so unkind."

"Unkind? Whatever are you talking about Richard?"

She seemed genuinely shocked and he paused. Had he misunderstood her? "Ah...I'm not sure. What are you talking about?"

"Why, that you've finally hit the jackpot."

"The jackpot?"

"Yes. Now that I've met her, I can tell you that I was beginning to despair of your ever being attracted to a...dece—of your bringing an acceptable woman home."

"Decent? You mean you...you like her?"

"Like her? What an absolutely strange question. Why wouldn't I like her, Richard? She seems to be a perfectly lovely woman. I don't wonder that you were about to take her to bed at this early hour."

"Take her to bed? Mom—"

"Yes, Richard, to bed. You are sleeping with her." She frowned. "Or should I ask if you're...fucking her?"

"No, you shouldn't," he said shortly.

She looked him. "Now you're annoyed. Well, don't be. I just never know what to call making love anymore. When they thought I was out of earshot on their last visit, I heard Jerry and Bettie whispering about going home and fucking like bunnies."

He suppressed a smile. His younger brother by two years, Jerry, and his wife had two teenage boys and had just celebrated their sixteenth wedding anniversary. "What's wrong with just calling it making love?"

"All right, dear. Are you making love to her regularly?"

He stared at her silently for several moments. "Mom, I love you dearly."

She gave him a satisfied smile. "I should hope so. I'm your mother, dear."

"But I'd just as soon not discuss my sex life with you."

"Oh, well, I expect that's normal. Still, I hope it's not just physical, Richard, dear. Your Jennifer is perfectly lovely. I can see you're eager to get back to her, so I'll say good night and you two can get on with taking care of business."

"Mom!"

"Oh, don't bother denying that you were about to take her to bed," she told him.

True to her word, once back in the living room, his mother made her excuses and breezed out the door. He walked her to her car and leaned in to kiss her cheek. "Drive carefully, Mom."

"I always do, dear. I'm sure I don't have to tell you to enjoy yourself," she said, smiling at him. "I'm sure you'll be getting all the loving you want or need tonight."

"Mom! Come on," he protested, feeling himself blush.

She started her engine. "I'm leaving, dear. Let the loving begin."

Chapter Nine

Jennifer was pacing the floor in front of the living room door when he went back inside. She turned to look at him. "Okay. Tell me: what did she say about me? Be honest. I can handle it."

He arched a brow. "Are you sure?"

She blanched. "It was that bad?" She lifted her chin. "Yes. So what did she want to know? Why you weren't with a beautiful, slender blonde?"

He smiled. "What an imagination you have. As it happens, she was quite taken with you. She told me it was time I started dating a decent woman. It seems she thinks the women I've been dating so far have been bimbos."

She grinned at him, visibly relaxing her shoulders. "Partial to bimbos, are you?"

"I'm partial to you. And so, apparently, is my mother. She implied you were quite a cut above my normal hussy."

She narrowed her gaze and gave him a mock frown. "Normal hussy? Would you like to rephrase that, buddy? Sounds like you're implying I'm an abnormal hussy. If you are, you should know that that's a surefire way to ensure you get to spend a long, sexless night alone."

He laughed and tipped up her chin. "Then I definitely didn't mean that. I want...I need to spend the night making love to you."

She smiled and leaned against him. "Now that's better. Although there is something I'd like even more than making love to and with you."

"What could you possibly like more than making love?" he teased, cupping her breasts in his hands.

"Only one thing."

She suddenly sounded shy and he was intrigued. "And that is?"

"I want to be fucked."

"Fucked?"

"Yes. Fucked. Hard. I want you to slam your cock into my pussy — over and over. I want you to tear my pussy up. I want to be fucked so hard that I see stars."

He watched her cheeks redden, but was pleased that she didn't look away from him. "Hard and fast, huh?"

"Yes. Will you fuck me, Rick?"

"Damn straight, I will!"

He slipped his arms around her and she pressed her hands against his chest. "I want to be fucked hard...but not rough. I don't like rough sex."

He tipped up her chin and pressed his lips against hers in a long, needy kiss. "Don't worry. I don't do rough sex. I aim to please you, not bruise you. Well, maybe your pussy will feel a little bruised afterwards, but that's what you want. Isn't it?"

"Yes. Fuck me raw."

She stroked her fingers through his hair and whispered his name.

He resisted the urge to undress her in the living room and led her through the house to his bedroom. He dimmed the lights, turned on his bedroom stereo, and slowly undressed her. Gazing down at her nude body, as she stood shyly in front of him, he wondered again why some lucky man hadn't snatched her up a long time ago.

"You are such a beautiful woman," he told her as he urged her on to the side of his bed. He undressed quickly. Catching her gaze, he stood in front of her with a condom in his hand. "Think you can handle it this time?" he teased.

She nodded silently and eagerly reached for him. The feel of her soft hands holding him sent a burst of lust down his cock and to his balls.

To his surprised delight, instead of immediately sheathing him, she leaned forward and kissed the head of his dick. He sucked in a sharp breath. It had been a very long time since he'd had a blowjob or even had his cock kissed. He knew she wasn't going to suck him, but just having her kiss him like that made him even harder. She slowly rolled the rubber over his dick and fondled his balls.

She looked up at him, her dark eyes gleaming. "Oh, Rick, I love touching you like this. You have such nice balls, warm and heavy."

The desire to fuck her vanished. She was so beautiful and sweet. "We're going to have to take a rain check on that fucking," he warned her.

"Why?" Her eyes widened. She snatched her hands away from his sac. "Did I squeeze too hard? Did I hurt you?"

"No. No," he assured her. "I just want to make love to you tonight. Is that all right?"

She cupped his balls in her palm and lightly raked her fingertips over them. "Yes. I just want you inside me, Rick. But you'll owe me a fuck?"

"Yes. Count on it, honey." He lay on his back and watched as she lowered herself on him. He sighed with pleasure when her pussy closed over the tip of his cock. He bit his lip and clenched a hand into a fist to help ward off the urge to grab her hips and yanked them down until her hot, moist pussy surrounded and caressed his entire cock.

"Hmm." She smiled and licked her lips. "That feels good. So good, Rick." She lifted her hips, leaving only half his dick covered with pussy.

He lifted his hips slightly. "Jenn…"

"Oh. Somebody wants more pussy?" she demanded.

"Oh, God, yes. Now!"

"More pussy coming up, lover." She rotated her hips and thrust herself down until his entire shaft was pulsing into her again. She made a small, incoherent sound and ground against him.

He felt a shock of desire, lust, and pleasure coil in his gut and throb through his cock. He wrapped his arms around her and pulled her down so that he could feel her soft breasts against his chest. "Make love to me, Jenn," he whispered.

"Oh, yes, Rick." She curled her fingers into his hair, brushed her breasts against his chest, and began raining kissed on his eager lips. "Oh, Rick. Rick! This is so good...I've never felt like this with anyone else...your cock...your lips...oh, God you're a sweet, delicious man!"

Feelings of joy and pleasure engulfed him. He closed his eyes and allowed his thoughts to drift. He lay underneath her thrusting body and clenching pussy, enjoying being made love to. He had never felt such a need and a passion for any other woman. What was happening to him went beyond wanting sex with her. Having her make love to him felt like something he'd waited his entire life to experience. And damn, but it had been worth the wait, he thought distractedly as he groaned, shuddered, and exploded inside her.

Even as he came, she lay on him, still kissing and touching him, clamping her tight pussy onto his spewing cock. He felt the tremors in her pussy increase and intensify. She moaned, suddenly and bit into his shoulder. He thrust up into her. Wetting a finger, he pressed against her tight, puckered butt. She whimpered, pressing her warm ass against his hand. He slipped his finger in her behind and began finger fucking her.

She sobbed with pleasure and her pussy finally detonated.

Still sobbing and trembling with pleasure, she pressed her cheek against his shoulder.

He stroked his hands down her sweat-covered back. "It's all right, honey. It's all right."

"Oh, God...oh, God..."

"That was one of the most satisfying fucks I've ever had," he told her.

"Yeah. It was rather good, wasn't it?" she asked, sounding pleased.

"Yes."

They lay together with the sound of soft jazz providing a soothing backdrop to their satisfied passion. Lying there with her breasts pressed against his chest, he felt content and...happy. This might not be a bad way to spend the rest of his life. He fell asleep with her soft hands stroking over his chest. He could definitely become addicted to this and her.

* * * * *

Jennifer stared at the man standing next to her mother in disbelief. He was tall, lean, brown-eyed and looked like the boy next door. He had thick dark hair and didn't look much older than Rick. Watching him look at her slender, still beautiful mother, she saw the same look of desire on his face as she saw on Rick's when he looked at her.

"Jenny, honey, this is Paul Westerfield. Paul, this is my baby, Jenny."

He smiled. "Hello, Jennifer. I've heard so many wonderful things about you from Helen. It's a pleasure to meet you."

She nodded silently, still staring wide-eyed at her mother and her boyfriend.

"Well, Jenny, I know our visit is unexpected, but are you going to invite us in, or are you hiding a man in there?" Her mother asked, laughing lightly.

Jennifer forced a smile. Her mother didn't know that Rick had left just ten minutes earlier. "I'm sorry. I was just having coffee. Come in."

"Coffee sounds great."

In the kitchen, she saw her mother's gaze on the two coffee cups on the counter and steeled herself to answer endless questions. To her amazement, her mother merely gave her a knowing smile and looked away.

"I know it's rather early for a visit, but I thought it was time you and Paul met," her mother told her as she poured coffee for them. "We're going away for a week-long stay down at Ocean City. Paul wanted to call first, but I told him you wouldn't mind a quick, unannounced visit."

If they had come a half an hour earlier, they'd have interrupted her and Rick's early morning quickie. "You're going to spend a week together? In the same room?" she asked, feeling her cheeks burn.

"Yes," her mother answered calmly. "We're both adults, Jenny." She glanced at the two cups on the counter. "I'm sure you understand."

"It's not the same thing," she said defensively. Although there were eleven years separating her and Rick, the age difference was in the right direction.

"It's exactly the same thing, Jennifer," her mother countered. "And we didn't come here for your approval. We came so you two could be introduced. I think we'll be moving along now. Have a good day, Jenny."

She followed them to her apartment door. "Mom, wait a minute. I'm sorry. I just need a little time to adjust. It's only been ten months since—"

"I don't need to be reminded how long it been since your father's death, Jennifer."

She saw the pain in her mother's eyes and wished she had been more gracious. "I'm sorry, Mom." She hugged her mother. "Come back for a visit when you return home?"

"Both of us?"

"Yes." She released her mother and looked up at Paul. "I'll see you both in a week or so."

He nodded. "I do understand your reluctance to—"

"She'll have to get over her reluctance," her mother interrupted.

She walked them to the elevator before going back to her apartment. She had needlessly made her mother unhappy and that was unforgivable. Her parents had been married for just over thirty years when he father had died as a result of injuries suffered in a car crash. Her mother had been inconsolable during the months following her father' death — until she'd met Paul at a gas station.

Now she seemed happy and content. She would learn to deal with her mother's relationship with Paul just as she'd expect her mother to deal with hers with Rick, if they ever actually had one.

They had spent the last month going to ballgames, dancing at jazz clubs, having dinner out, and she'd even managed to drag him to the mall to shop twice. During that time, he'd never let more than two days pass without calling or seeing her. They alternated between spending the occasional night at her apartment and his house. She frowned. Still, she didn't know how he felt about her. Or even if he felt anything other than desire. She knew she felt so much more than that for him.

* * * * *

"She's really starting to piss me off."

Troy sighed and ran both hands through his hair. "You and me both, but we really need to pull out all the stops to get this account."

Rick, sprawling on the sofa in Troy's office, swore. "What the hell does she want anyway?"

"Actually, Rick, I'm beginning to think she's stalling."

"Why should she stall?"

"I think she likes going out with you."

He sat up and stared at Troy. "What?"

"It makes sense, Rick. No matter how closely we follow the specs she gives us, she finds a need for more revisions and only wants to discuss them over a meal. And then only with you."

"Only with me?"

"Yes. When I called her two weeks ago to tell her I had several questions and suggested we meet for a meal, she insisted on discussing the changes over the phone. When I called her to tell her we'd made the changes, she insisted on discussing them over dinner. When I told her I'd have to check my schedule and get back to her, she said not to bother. That I should have your secretary call to set up a dinner meeting between the two of you. It's obvious that she's attracted to you. What about you?"

"What about me?"

"Are you attracted to her?"

"Hell, no!"

Troy leaned back in his chair. "No? She's very attractive, auburn hair, beautiful body. What is it that you're not attracted to?"

"Her. She's not my type. I told you, Troy, I don't go for skinny, flat-chested, no ass women anymore, even if you do."

Troy shook his head. "I'm not attracted to her or any woman other than Angie." He smiled suddenly. "Do you know that Angie gets sweeter every day? Shit, I love and adore that woman more now than I did before we got married."

Rick fought off the now familiar feeling of envy he always felt when he was with Troy and Angie or even when Troy talked about how much he loved her. That's how he was beginning to feel about Jennifer. How he wanted her to feel about him.

"I'm not interested in Connie Betton. If you think we have no chance to win the account, I'll be happy to tell her to fuck off."

Troy laughed. "I think that's what she wants — to fuck you."

"Well if that's what it'll take to land the account, it's lost to us."

"Why?"

"Why? Are you nuts? You expect me to fuck her to land the account?"

"Expect it?" Troy shook his head. "No, but I admit that I am a little surprised at your outright refusal."

"Why?"

"Why? I've known you to take two women to bed and think nothing of it."

"That was over four years ago," he said, recalling that he'd spent most of the cruise where Troy and Angie had met, sleeping with two, beautiful, well-built blondes. It was also before he'd met Jennifer. "There's no way I'm fucking a woman for any reason other than that she turns me on, and that leaves Connie Betton out."

"Why don't you bring her over for dinner one night?"

"Bring her over for dinner? Why?"

"Angie would love to meet her."

"Why?" he asked again, narrowing his gaze.

"Because she knows you're seeing her and she's been dropping subtle hints that she'd like to meet her."

"Troy, I am not 'seeing' Connie Betton and if Angie is so eager to meet her, no one's stopping you from taking her home for dinner."

Troy's brows arched and he laughed. "We have our wires crossed. I meant why don't you bring Jennifer over for dinner."

"Oh. Jennifer."

"Yes. Jennifer. When do we get to meet her?"

He shook his head. "I don't know. Soon…maybe…if things continue to go…all right."

"Why shouldn't they?"

He shrugged. "I don't know. I think she's finally starting to trust me and to realize that I am for real."

"Ah. Ready to admit that you're in love with her?"

"No," he said shortly. He hadn't admitted that, even to himself, but only because he didn't want to get hurt. And if she didn't share his feelings, he was going to be in for the biggest heartache of his life. "What are we going to do about Connie Betton?"

"Everything short of your fucking her that we can. We could really use that account, Rick."

He sighed. "I know that, but I am not fucking her."

"Afraid Jennifer will find out?"

He shook his head. "I don't want to fuck her. She doesn't do anything for me, but if it's at all humanly possibly to land the account without fucking her, I'll do it. If she wants to be wined and dined, I'll wine and dine her, but without any hint of romance. No flowers, no phone calls just to say hi, and no touching or kissing. Anything else, it's up for grabs."

Troy nodded. "That's all I asked. Give it all you can without doing anything to endanger your relationship with Jennifer."

He glanced at his watch and rose. "Speaking of Jennifer, we have a date tonight. I'm heading out. See you tomorrow."

Four hours later, he and Jennifer walked hand in hand along the riverfront after dinner and dancing. He listened quietly while she told him of her mother's unexpected visit earlier than day.

She fell silent and turned to look up at him. "I'm going to have to accept their relationship, but it's going to take some time. Every time I looked at him, I couldn't help feeling he'd never be able to fill my dad's shoes."

Although troubled, her silver eyes were even more alluring by the light of the moon. He brushed a hand against her cheek. "Maybe not as your dad, but surely it's up to your mother to decide if he can fill your father's place in her life."

She sighed and burrowed into him, slipping her arms around him. "I know. I sound like an overgrown spoiled brat, I know."

"No, you don't. My father's been dead for ten years and I keep expecting my mother to turn up with a lover. If she ever does, I'll probably feel the same way you do. It can't be easy to make such a big adjustment in much a short time."

"I think that's part of the problem. Less than a year ago, my dad was alive and healthy and they were happy. Now she has this young stud who looks at her as if he can't wait to get her alone so he can fuck her."

He gave her a hug and pressed his lips against her hair in silent sympathy.

They stood, holding each other in silence for several moments before they walked on. "Speaking of fucking," he said casually. "I believe you owe me one."

She turned to look up at him. "Do you aim to collect tonight?"

"Yeah, baby," he drawled and they both laughed.

"And this time, Jenn, I am going to fuck you. Not make love to you, but fuck your pussy. There won't be any Jenn or Rick, just hungry pussy and greedy cock."

"You're making me wet all ready."

"That's the idea. You're going to need to be very wet because I intend to fuck the shit out of you."

She stretched up to kiss him. "Then let's go home and let the fucking began."

He slipped his arms around her waist. "Your place or mine?"

"Mine. I want you to fuck me in my own bed."

Chapter Ten

Kneeling on all fours on her king-sized bed with Rick naked behind her, Jennifer shivered with anticipation. It had been ages since she'd had a no-holds-barred outright fucking for fucking's sake.

Palming her breasts, he leaned over and bit the back of her neck. "Are you sure about this?" he asked softly, his voice husky.

"Yes," she whispered, rubbing her rear against his cock. He was already fully aroused and sheathed. "I'm very sure."

He released his hold on one of her breasts and slipped two fingers into her already damp passage. "Your pussy's moist and creamy," he said.

"Tell me something I don't already know. Like when you're going to stop talking and start fucking," she complained, thrusting her behind back against him. "If you don't start cooperating soon, I'll be forced to take some cock by force."

He laughed softly, released his hold on her other breast, and holding her hips, he pushed the big head of his shaft into her.

"Hmm." She bit her bottom lip and closed her eyes. She breathed in deeply as they enjoyed what had lately become a delicious ritual for them: taking several moments to savor having the first few inches of his cock embedded in her.

"I think someone is ready to be stuffed full of hungry cock," he whispered, leaning over her to nibble at the back of her neck.

"Yeah?" She pushed her hips back, signaling her desire to be drilled. "You gonna talk or are you gonna fuck?" she demanded.

"I am definitely gonna fuck you."

"Hard," she encouraged.

"Very hard," he countered and began thrusting his big dick deep into her pussy.

She moaned and closed her eyes. "Oh, lord, Rick! Your cock feels so good. So good."

"So does your sweet pussy." He withdrew all but the big head of his cock from her before slamming back into her pussy with enough force to make her gasp.

"Oh! Oh, yeah, baby! That's it. That's it, baby! Harder. Let me feel your big balls slapping against my body. Oh, damn. Ream me, baby. Ream me hard. Drive that big monster deep in my pussy! Oooh! Oh, God, hurt me, baby! Hurt my pussy! Fuck the shit out of me!"

He gripped her hips in his hands and slammed his hips against hers, sending his cock plowing deep within her, making them both gasp and shudder with pleasure. "Oh, Jenn, honey, you are so sweet and so beautiful. I don't know which I love more…making love to you or fucking your cunt. They both turn me on and make me so hard and hot. Damn, you are the sweetest woman I've ever met.

"Here, baby! Take my cock! Take all of it up your pussy! Here I am again!" His hard groin smashed against her ass, driving his lust-laden dick, cleaving through her pussy and into her soul.

Oh, God almighty!

It was as if his cock had taken on a life of its own. It slammed into her over and over again, until it began to hurt. The furious motion of his shaft burrowing in and out of her at an incredible pace eroded her ability to speak. Her whole body was hot, her pussy the center of her universe. Having him make love to her was sweet, having her pussy fucked raw like this by a man she adored was wonderful beyond words.

Clenching her breasts in his palms, he pummeled her pussy with hard, desperate strokes. The floodgates of paradise burst open, and unable to hold off her orgasm any longer, she moaned and shuddered helplessly. Her knees and arms gave out and she fell forward on to her stomach, still filled to the brink with hard, throbbing dick.

Moving his hands from her breasts to her hips, he followed her down and continued ramming his cock deep into her climaxing pussy. He rotated his powerful hips, withdrew all but the head of his big cock, and slammed it back into her cunt.

"Aaahhh!" She moaned and clenched her teeth on the pillow. "Oh, God! No more, Rick! Please. It's too good."

He wrapped his arms around her shoulders and fucked her hard and rough, making her whole body shudder. "Just a little more, baby! Just let me have a little more of your pussy! Spread your legs wider. Lift your hips. Let me get all the way up in your pussy!"

The pleasure-pain was intense. She gritted her teeth and kept her eyes closed as he relentlessiy fucked her already sated cunt.

"Oh, damn! Oooh, damn! God dammit!" he groaned, called out her name, and exploded inside her.

He collapsed onto to her, his cock still buried up her now sore pussy.

She lay under him, listening to the sound of his deep, uneven breathing. She loved the feel of his heart thumping against her.

They lay still joined for several, quiet minutes, regaining their breaths.

"Oh, Jenn, honey, that was good," he moaned, lying on top of her, his cheek pressed against hers.

She laughed softly. "It was way beyond good. That's some fucking cock you have there."

"It's only as good as the pussy it's ravishing," he said, his voice warm and deep. "And you have the best pussy I've ever had."

"Oh, Rick!"

He bit her neck. "So you think you'll want to fuck instead of make love again?"

"Lord, I thought you were going to literally fuck the shit out of me, but yes."

He laughed. "Next time," he promised.

She turned her head and puckered her lips.

He brushed his mouth against hers. "You make me so hot, Jenn."

"And hard too," she laughed.

"That too," he agreed. "Lying here with my cock still in your sweet pussy, I feel more content than I've ever felt."

Her heart thumped and she sucked in a breath. He sounded as if he meant that. "Me too, Rick," she admitted. "You make me cream like no other man ever has. Must be that big cock of yours."

"You like big cocks?"

"Yes…especially when they're attached to big, handsome, blond men."

"Since when do you like blonds?" he teased.

"Since I met you," she said.

"Does that mean you're ready to trust me, Jenn?"

"Yes. Please don't hurt me, Rick."

Rick felt as if he'd just won a ticket to the Super Bowl. To have her finally ready to trust him was a heady sensation. If all it took to gain her trust was fucking her, he should have done it weeks earlier. "Oh, baby, I won't." He kissed her lips gently. "You can trust me, Jenn."

She made a small, incoherent sound and tightened her pussy around his cock. Seemed she wanted to be fucked again. Well, he was more than happy and ready to oblige.

He lifted off her and rolled onto his back. That's when he realized that he was no longer wearing the condom. He scrambled to his knees and looked at her, expecting to see it her on ass cheeks. When it wasn't there, he leaned over and gently urged her legs apart.

When it wasn't on the bed between her thighs, his heart thumped. There was only one other place it could be.

"What's wrong?" she asked.

He sighed and touched her cunt. "Jenn...ah...there's been an accident."

"What? What kind of accident?" she sat up and looked at him, her eyes wide.

"The condom...it's still in you."

She blinked at him and stared at his bare cock. "In me?"

"It must have come off when I came."

"Then...that means...you...you came in me and not it in."

"Damn. I'm sorry."

She looked stunned and a little frightened, and he knew she would be thinking of a possible unwanted pregnancy. He urged her onto her back, spread her legs, and inserted his fingers in her pussy. He located the condom just inside her. From what he could tell, it didn't seem to contain any semen. He carefully removed it from her.

She sat up and turned the lights up. They both stared at it. Although the outside was covered with their combined juices, the inside was relatively dry. He had ejaculated into her rather than it.

To his dismay, his cock became hard at the thought that he had fucked her and ejaculated directly into her pussy. From conversations they'd had earlier on, he knew she was allergic to birth control pills. Their sole method of birth control and safe sex had consisted of his religiously wearing a condom when they made love.

She turned and buried her face against her pillow.

He lay down behind her and kissed her neck. "I'm sorry. I didn't realize I wasn't wearing it until I went to remove it."

"I cannot afford to get pregnant," she said.

He dipped his finger in her pussy, moistened it, and then eased it up her tight ass. "Why not?"

"Why not?" She turned to face him, squirming as he gently fingered her behind. "It may be old-fashioned of me, but I want to be married *before* I get pregnant, thank you very much!"

"It was an accident, Jenn. You don't think I did it on purpose...do you?"

"No, of course not. Why would you? I know you're no more eager to get me pregnant than I am to get pregnant."

He bit back the urge to contradict her. The thought of her having his baby was a definite turn on. He felt his cock stirring again. He withdrew his finger from her ass to the tip before pushing it gently back in her.

"Hmm. Rick!"

"Somebody is beginning to enjoy having her ass reamed."

"Only with your fingers. Rick, I really am not into the thought of having you try to get your cock up my ass."

"That's all right, Jenn. I'm content with your pussy, especially now that I know you won't object to the occasional slam house fuck."

"Slam house fuck? Whatever you call it, I loved it...even though it started to hurt near the end."

He frowned. "Did you want me to stop?"

"Not on your life, buster! I wouldn't have stopped you for a million bucks."

"Good. I like a woman who, although ladylike most of the time, can appreciate a little raunchiness." He kissed her, still gently fucking her ass. "Jenn...we've already risked a possible pregnancy once." He touched her breast. "If you're pregnant, you need to know, you won't be in it alone. I'll be with you every step of the way and it goes without saying that I will be a responsible father, emotionally and financially."

She stared at him. "You sound as if the idea wouldn't bother you."

He shook his head. "Why should it? I want kids. Who better to be the mother of my child than the woman I adore?"

"My being pregnant wouldn't bother you at all?"

"No. Actually, I kind of like the idea."

"You're serious."

"Yes. Jenn, your being pregnant wouldn't be the end of the world. Would it?"

"No, but…no…but…"

"But what?"

She shook her head. "No."

"I think we should increase the chances of your getting pregnant."

"What?"

He removed his finger from her ass.

The small sound of protest she made, brought a smile to his face. He eased her onto her back and slid his body on top of hers. "Just in case you're not pregnant, I think we should repeat the offense."

She pushed against his shoulders and he lifted his upper body so he could look down into her eyes. "What?"

"What do you think you're doing?"

"I'm about to make love to you," he whispered.

"Rick, wait! My…my pussy is a little raw. You gave it an incredible pounding."

"I said make love, not fuck." He urged her thighs apart and pressed his cock against the entrance of her pussy. "Without a condom."

She shook her head. "That's not a good idea, Rick."

"It's a great idea." He reached between their bodies to rub the head of his cock against her pussy. "If you're already pregnant, no harm will be done."

"And if I'm not?"

"If you're not, we'll repeat the offense until you are."

"Rick...I've never done this before."

"Done what?"

"Been with a man without a condom."

He stared at her. "Never?"

"Never. I...I was a virgin until my freshman year of college and by that time I knew enough to insist on a condom."

"I haven't made love to a woman without a condom since my senior year of high school. This is going to be doubly sweet for us both, honey." He pushed gently, easing the head of his dick between the lips of her pussy. He paused, giving her time to insist that he stop and don a condom.

Instead, she took a deep breath, closed her eyes, and arched her back. He pressed forward. With his cock, half way inside her, he froze, a feeling of absolute delight washing over him. He had never felt anything this good or right in his life. Then, unable to resist any longer, he pushed forward until his entire shaft was inside her warm, creamy body.

He found her mouth and began kissing her. He had planned to make love to her, but she soon made it clear she wanted to do a little love making of her own. She shoved at his shoulders until he rolled over to his back with her on top of him.

"Rick?"

"Yes, honey?"

"I love your cock."

"I love your pussy, baby."

"Let me show you show much."

He smiled. He loved that she touched, kissed, caressed, and whispered to him. He was a marvelous lover...she loved his tight, firm ass...his chest pressing against her tits made her nipples hard...she loved feeling his big cock in her pussy...his cock was the best she'd ever had...she never wanted him to take it out of her pussy...he made her hot...she needed him and his dick...she wanted to be filled with his come...

Unable to bear the pleasure building up in him, he rolled her over on her back and began fucking her hard. When he felt her shuddering and whimpering under him, he released his tight grip on his control, thrust harder, and blasted his load directly into her sweet, hot, unprotected pussy. Oh, God. Paradise. Pure and simple.

They made love once more before falling asleep. He woke in the middle of the night. After returning from the bathroom, he pulled the cover off her, urged her from her side onto her stomach, and kneeling between her legs, he began kissing her big, gorgeous ass. He licked the mounds, fondling them, loving the way they jiggled. God, she had a nice ass. He parted her cheeks and planted a kiss directly against her tight little hole. One of these days, he was going to fuck her ass with more than his finger.

She moaned in her sleep and he resisted the urge to stick his tongue in her ass. Although her ass was fast becoming an obsession with him, she was not ready for it to be fucked. He gently eased her on her back and transferred his attentions to her front. Smiling, he began fingering her pussy. It was caked with their combined fluids and smelled of stale sex and her juices. His nostrils flared and he jabbed his tongue against her clit.

She moaned and came awake. "Rick? What are you doing?"

"Having a midnight snack," he told her. He pushed at her ass until she lifted it, then he put a pillow under it. "Go back to sleep."

"While you have all the fun? Dream on, Rick. Now stop talking, and do something constructive with that tongue of yours."

He willingly obliged, stroking his tongue into her much like it was his cock. His senses were overwhelmed by the smell and heat of her aroused pussy. His cock hardened and he felt as if his nuts were about to bust but he kept kissing, touching, and sinking his tongue in her until she moaned, shuddered.

He parted the lips of her cunt and gently inserted two fingers in her. Locking his mouth on her clit, he leisurely finger fucked her, reveling in her moans and heated words of lust.

"Oh, lord, Rick, that feels so…oooh…that's it. Oh, my lord, that's it, Rick. Yes. Ooooh, yes! Yes!" she moaned and came against his tongue. Clutching her thighs, he buried his face against her cunt and eagerly lapped at her fragrant bush. He leisurely dipped his tongue into her creaming warmth, savoring the taste of her on his tongue before swallowing. Damn, he'd never tasted anything as hot as her pungent pussy juices.

With his cock hard and throbbing, he collapsed on the bed beside her. She delighted him by pushing him onto his back, and impaling herself on him.

"Oh, my God, this is so damn good. God, Jennifer, you intoxicate me. You are so sweet…so sexy. Your pussy is unbearably hot and enticing. I could happily spend the rest of my life, eating and fucking it."

"Yeah, right. I know you're plotting to get your jackhammer cock up my ass, but it ain't gonna happen, buddy. Ever."

He laughed, undeterred. Ever was a long time and she'd already come to love having several of his fingers up her tight ass. He was confident that one day, she'd welcome his cock there. He could be patient until she was ready to discover the real joys of anal sex.

He kissed her lips. "You'd better resign yourself to getting pregnant."

"Why is that?" she asked breathlessly as she rode up and down on his cock. She teased him by repeatedly lifting her hips until all but his lucky cock head was outside her body, before abruptly slamming her cunt down the length of his dick. Then she would grind her hips in a circular motion, allowing her inner muscles to caress and massage his cock. Before he could shove his hips up and begin fucking into her, she would lift herself again, leaving only his cock head inside the entrance of her cunt. She repeated this offense again and again, driving him wild with the need to get a few deep, hard pumps up into her teasing channel.

Enough. He wanted a good fuck. He wrapped his arms around her waist, slammed her down onto his cock, and shot his dick up into her. She moaned and shuddered. He smiled and fucked her harder, using short, greedy thrusts to spare her pussy. Damn, her pussy was good! "There's no way I can give this up…oh, God…no way…it's too good…too sweet…God, I'm drunk with wanting you."

Feeling his climax gathering like a storm on the horizon, he sucked a full, ripe breast in his mouth, and fucked her wildly. He loved how her ass jiggled against his thighs and her breast bobbled in his mouth. Her soft wails fueled his desire and he sped up, propelling his cock into her so hard, a feeling akin to pain accompanied his mounting passion.

She shuddered and clung to him as she came again. Sinking his teeth into her large, luscious breast, he followed quickly, gasping as he blew his load into her unprotected pussy. She moaned and tumbled on him, her pussy still cradling and holding his cock.

He kissed her shoulder, stroking his fingers through her thick, dark hair. "I need you to do something for me, Jenn."

"What?"

"Be my woman."

She lifted her head briefly to look at him. "I've been your woman for weeks. It's time you realized you were my man."

"For as long as you want me," he promised.

"I don't share," she warned him. "If you're mine…you're all mine."

"All yours, honey. You can't possibly think I want any other woman."

"Good, because I don't want any other man, Rick." She settled against his shoulder. "Just you."

He stroked his hands over her body and felt a quiet satisfaction. They were slowly getting closer to the time when she was ready to surrender her heart to him. He kissed her shoulder. "Just you," he echoed.

After she fell asleep, he lay drowsy and content, thinking about her and their future together. For the first time in his life, he could fully envision being happy and satisfied with just one woman.

* * * * *

"How's it going with Blondie?"

Jennifer paused in the act of making another sketch of Rick and looked at Cherica, who lounged in a folding lawn chair on the grass a few feet to her right. Instead of spending their Saturday afternoon shopping, she and Cherica had decided to pack a picnic lunch and head for a small park two miles from their apartment complex.

She shrugged. "Okay...actually, I think...I could really go for him."

"No shit, Sherlock. I could have told you that when you plunked down five big ones for a date with him...how long has it been?"

"Since we met? A little over four months."

"He still ringing your bell?"

"Rica, I think he'll still be ringing my bell when we're both old and feeble."

"Wow. That sounds...semi-serious. You two serious?"

"Serious? I don't know. We're not going out with anyone else and we've stopped using protection, so I guess—"

Cherica bolted up in her lounger so quickly it nearly toppled over. She whipped off her sunglasses and stared at her. "What? Did I hear you right? Did you just say you're not using protection?"

She sighed. "Yes, I did." She held up her hands, palms out. "Okay, Rica. Don't freak."

Cherica took a deep breath and sounded calmer when she spoke again. "Jenn. You think that's a wise move? I know he's a big, good-looking guy, but do you really want to risk getting pregnant?"

"I think he'd like that. As a matter of fact, I know he would. He wants to settle down."

"Settle down? Has he proposed?"

"No," she admitted, recalling her disappointment when she had told him she wanted to be married before she got pregnant. She had hoped it would trigger an offer to marry her if that happened. Granted it wouldn't have been as welcome as a marriage proposal freely and spontaneously given, but she would still have accepted it. "But I know he wants me to have his baby."

"And you're willing to oblige a man who doesn't want to marry you?"

She flushed. "Rica, you're making me sound like an idiot and him like a heel. It's not like that. He's kind, considerate, romantic, and I know that he has feelings for me that go beyond the sex."

"Really? How considerate is it of him to subject you to an unwanted pregnancy just so he can come in you?"

"Who says it would be unwelcome?"

"I do. I know you, Jenn. Don't bother telling me you wouldn't have a problem with being unmarried and pregnant."

How could she explain how she felt when she was with him? True, the idea of being pregnant and unmarried held little appeal, but she knew he would stand by her, as he'd said. And maybe she was just being hopelessly out of date thinking marriage had to come before the babies did.

She shrugged. "I'll deal with it, if I have to."

"If you have to? Jenn, you keep letting him bang you without a condom it's bound to happen. What am I missing? Why do you let him touch you without protection?"

"The first time it happened it was an accident."

"I don't know how you accidentally make love without protection, but okay, I'll buy that the first time was an accident. What about the next time?"

"Don't look at me like that. I know it's not wise, but he wanted it so much and so did I."

"Yeah, Jenn, we'd all like to be able to fuck without protection, but it's not practical or safe."

She shook her head. "I know all that, but Rica, you have no idea how...how addictive having his bare cock inside me has become. I feel like a junkie. I've never felt anything like it. I can't give it up. He enchants me. He says my pussy is intoxicating and that he gets high every time we make love. And so do I."

Rica shook her head. "I don't believe this. I do not believe this. Jenn! Wake up and smell the coffee! You can't keep sleeping with him without protection. What if you two break up? Are you really prepared to be a single parent?"

"Even if we break up, he'd do his part for the baby, both emotionally and financially."

"And that would make it all right?"

Maybe not, but it would certainly make being a single parent a hell of a lot easier. "He wants a baby, Rica...and I'm inclined to want to have his baby."

Cherica shook her head. "Okay. Fine. I know that look. I think you're being incredibly shortsighted, but I can see your mind's made up. What can I do?"

"Just be there for me."

"Always, Jenn. You know that."

She nodded. Her period was a week late. She would need Cherica's support. Just in case Rick, who she was seeing less and less of, let her down. She couldn't share her biggest fear with Cherica: that Rick was growing tired of her.

"Thanks."

Cherica waved a hand in dismissal. "So what are your plans for tonight? You want to have a girl's night out?"

"Actually, we have tentative plans."

"Tentative plans? Why tentative? He works for himself and he certainly doesn't work on the weekends."

"Not normally, but lately everyone at his firm has been working a lot of overtime in an effort to bring in this big account."

"I thought you said he did very little designing himself."

"I did, but...there are all kinds of details to be worked out." She realized how defensive she sounded and paused. "He's been working a lot of OT lately."

"Okay. How about tomorrow night?"

"Well...I'd like to, but if things don't work out tonight, we're going to go out tomorrow to dinner and dancing."

"I see. Okay." She smiled suddenly. "You know, Jenn, I think it's going to be all right with you and Blondie."

She forced a smile. "I hope so because I'm sort of...fond of him."

"Well, I'm sure he's just as...fond of you, Jenn."

God, she hoped so.

Her phone was ringing as she got home a few hours later. She rushed across the room and snatched up the cordless phone. "Hello."

"Hi, honey."

"Rick. Are you on your way already? If you are, you're going to have to wait a bit. I just got back from the park. I need to wash my hair, shower, and decide what I'm wearing. Where are we going?"

"Tonight? Unfortunately nowhere. Honey, I have to work."

"Again?" This was the fourth time in two weeks he'd cancelled a date with her.

"I know we had plans, but I really need to work tonight. And I have to go now."

"Will I see you later?"

"I probably won't finish until late."

She resisted the urge to say she didn't mind how late he came. God, why had she become so needy and clingy just as his passion for her was cooling at a frightening pace? Obviously, he was trying to let her down slowly as he broke off their relationship.

"Listen, honey, I have to go. I'll call you tomorrow."

"Okay."

"Good night."

"Yeah," she said and gently placed the phone on the receiver. She looked in the mirror over the phone table. Her eyes were wide and scared and her face ashen. "You'd better get ready to be dumped," she told her reflection. "And you'd better pray that you are not pregnant because he clearly is not going to support you emotionally."

She turned away from the mirror, her eyes filling with tears. She was a hopeless case, falling for another blond who didn't want her after the novelty wore off. Well, she wasn't going to spend the night sitting around feeling sorry for herself. She called Cherica.

"Jenn, you caught me as I was on my way to the shower."

"Shower? Going somewhere?"

"Yes. Jayson just called and asked me to have dinner with him."

"Okay. That's great."

"Jenn? Is something wrong? Shouldn't you be hitting the shower for your date with Blondie?"

"He just called. He can't make it."

"Oh. Ah...damn. Tell you want, you sound a little down. Why don't you join me and Jayson?"

"What? What happened to two's company?"

"That doesn't count with Jayson and me. He won't mind."

She shook her head. If Cherica didn't face reality soon, she was going to lose Jayson. "Maybe not, but I am not in the mood to be the third wheel."

"I'll call him back and tell him I can't make it, then you and I—"

"No! You go and have fun. I'm feeling...a little funky, but I'll be fine. We'll talk tomorrow."

"Jenn. Are you sure?"

"Positive. I'll have a quiet evening. Enjoy yourself," she said and hung up. "Well, Jenn, seems you'll have to paint the town on your own."

Determined not to waste the evening thinking about Rick, who apparently would rather work late at the office than take her out, she showered, put on her sexiest dress, and headed to her favorite jazz club.

Chapter Eleven

"This is nice."

Rick made an effort to keep what he hoped was a pleasant expression on his face as he looked across the restaurant table at Connie Betton. He no longer doubted that Troy was right about her interest in him being personal. As intelligent as she was, he marveled that she had yet to realize that he had not the slightest interest in her as a woman.

"Don't you think so?" she prodded when he remained silent.

The restaurant, located in one of the city's most upscale hotels, had very dim lighting, high backed booths, and a separate area for dancing. It had clearly been designed with lovers in mind. "Yes. Jennifer will love it."

Her smile vanished. "And who is Jennifer?"

"She's my lady."

"Your lady? Oh. I...didn't know you..."

"I'm sure you come here with your man," he said, deliberately. He'd had it with her and her damned games. He was tired of canceling dates with Jennifer so he could go out with her instead. It was time she understood that while Hunter and Markham's services were for sale, he was not.

"Actually, I'm not seeing anyone, Rick."

"Really? I'm surprised. Being involved in a very satisfying relationship, I can eagerly recommend it. There's nothing quite as fulfilling as having the right person in your life."

"I...see." She licked her lips and pushed her half eaten meal aside. "Ah...if you'll excuse me?"

He rose as she got up, grabbed her bag off the seat beside her, and hurried towards the restrooms.

He sank back in his seat. Well, he'd done it. When she came back, she would probably begin finding fault with the latest designs Troy and the design team had put in so much overtime to get ready for this dinner meeting. All their hard work would have been for nothing. All because he was selfish and wanted to spend more time with Jennifer. What would it have hurt him to see her a few more times?

He thought of all the dates with Jennifer he'd broken to see her and decided he'd done the right thing. If they lost the contract, so be it. There would be other opportunities that wouldn't require him to practically prostitute himself to land.

When she returned to the booth, she lifted her briefcase on to the table. "It's getting late. Why don't we take a look at the specs and see where we are?"

He pushed his own plate aside and lifted his briefcase onto the table. They spent the next forty minutes going over the specs. Finally, she sat back and looked at him. "What can I say? I think we have a workable plan."

He stared at her. "Excuse me?"

She gave him a cool smile. "I think Wilco's search for software designers has ended."

"We have the contract?"

"Yes." She nodded. "Hunter and Markham has earned it. Our lawyers will draw up the contract and we'll go from there." She glanced at her watch. "Well, I won't keep you from that lady of yours any longer."

Damn. He should have laid his cards on the table weeks earlier. He nodded and signaled the waiter to bring the check.

Outside the hotel where they'd met, he offered her his hand. He was surprised and annoyed when she abruptly linked her arms around his neck and pressed her mouth again his.

He jerked back and stared down at her. "What the hell was that all about?"

"Forgive me." She wiped her mouth. "I just had to have one kiss."

"Well, you've had it. Happy?"

She shook her head. "Your lady is one lucky woman."

"I'm very happily taken," he said coldly.

"I apologize. Good night," she said and hurried away.

He reluctantly followed her. He supposed he'd better make sure she got on her way safely. Once in her car, she waved to him.

He grudgingly waved back and headed toward his parking space. Finally, he would be able to spend more time with Jennifer. Hopefully, she'd soon begin to understand that he was completely serious about her. So serious, in fact, that it was becoming more difficult to refrain from asking her to marry him. He didn't think she trusted him enough to even consider becoming engaged to him. Always assuming, of course, that she loved him, which he readily admitted was a big assumption. If she loved him, wouldn't she automatically trust him not to hurt her?

Hell, even if she didn't trust him completely, he wanted to talk to her. In his car, he called her to tell her he'd finally landed the contract, but got her answering machine. Well, he'd get a bottle of champagne and they could celebrate when he saw her on the following day.

He called Troy with the news and headed home. Once there, he ordered two dozen red roses to be sent to Jennifer on the following morning.

* * * * *

On the way home from the club, Jennifer felt better. Not only had the music left her feeling mellow, but she'd danced several times with two men, both of whom had asked for her phone number. She'd refused, but just knowing that other men found her attractive helped lift her spirits.

Humming softly, she turned her car radio to the local news station. An accident on the interstate was causing a traffic nightmare. She'd have to take the long way home. She turned onto the road running along a wide street lined with hotels on one side and warehouses on another. As traffic ahead of her slowed, she came to a stop and idly glanced at the hotel to her right. She sucked in a breath and stared.

Rick, who was supposed to be working late, stood in front of the brightly lit building with what appeared to be a slender redhead. As she watched, the woman linked her arms around his neck and they began kissing.

Almost before they kiss had begun, he quickly drew away from the redhead. Jennifer sighed in relief. She'd misunderstood what she'd seen. Or had she? She bit her lip and her heart filled with despair. The woman was walking quickly away and he was eagerly following.

Several horns blaring behind her, forced her to drive on. She fought back tears and stared at the road in front of her, looking for a turn off. She found one half a mile away. She pulled onto a quiet street, turned off her engine, and sat with angry, hurt tears streaming down her cheeks.

Damn him! This was his idea of being her man? He had probably spent the evening fucking the redhead's unprotected pussy and telling her how she intoxicated him. Damn the lying, cheating bastard to hell! She gave an angry shake of her head and roughly wiped her tears away. She had been such a stupid cow! How had she convinced herself that she could keep him happy and content? Why would he settle for her when he could clearly have any woman he wanted?

Well, damn him, he could have them, but it would be a cold day in hell before she let him touch her again. Holding further tears at bay, she made the rest of the drive home. Once in her apartment, she sobbed in the shower. In her bed, she vowed to herself that she had shed her last tear over him.

She woke in the middle of the night with tears streaming down her cheeks. In the very short time that they had become regular lovers, she had foolishly surrendered her heart and soul to him. He had become such a part of her life. She looked forward to his calls and receiving unexpected flowers or balloons. She enjoyed watching ballgames with him, discussing sports, dancing with him, walking hand in hand along the beach or the waterfront with him. Even when they just lay in bed cuddling, she'd felt a level of belonging and caring that she had never felt for or with another man. She had let him into her life and told him things she'd never told another man.

Now he had betrayed her trust. She should hate him and never want to see him again, but the thought of never seeing him again was unbearable. Dismissing her pride, she decided that if he just apologized and promised it would never happen again, she would do her best to trust and forgive him.

Besides, she hadn't actually seen very much. Maybe she had misunderstood what little she'd seen. For all she knew, the woman might have been a long-time friend or even a cousin. Granted, she didn't kiss her friends of the opposite sex or her male cousins on the lips, but maybe some people did. Maybe he did.

She sucked in a deep, aching breath. No, that had not been a friendly or cousinly kiss. Nevertheless, maybe it hadn't meant anything. Maybe he'd just been horny and needed a quick release. That would hurt, but she could deal with him, as long as he could promise it wouldn't happen again.

* * * * *

Rick woke early the next morning, eager to see Jennifer. He had just finished packing an overnight bag when Angie called. "Come join us for a celebration brunch."

"I'd love to sweets, but I'm on my way to Jennifer's."

"Great. You know I've been dying to meet her. Bring her along."

He supposed it was time he introduced her to his friends. "Okay...if it's okay with her. If it's not we'll get together soon. Talk to you later, sweets."

He hung up and left the house. He hummed all the way to Jennifer's apartment. If she didn't have anything planned, maybe they could have dinner out after they left Angie and Troy's. Then they'd have all night together. Although he wanted to fuck her, maybe he'd resist the urge and just hold her...and hint at how he really felt about her and see how she reacted. If her reaction was positive...just maybe they'd soon be engaged.

When he arrived at Jennifer's apartment building, he rang her bell in the lobby several times with no response. He glanced at his watch. It was only seven fifty-five, so she must be home. He smiled suddenly. She was probably still asleep. She did like to sleep late. Not a month earlier, he'd suggested they exchange keys, but she'd insisted it was too early to take that step, so he'd dropped the subject.

He was just about to go to his car and listen to music for half an hour when she finally answered.

"Yes?"

"Hi, honey. It's me."

"Me?"

"Yes, me. It hasn't been that long since we saw each other." He smiled slightly and waited for a snappy comeback, but there was none. After several moments of silence, he heard the door release being sounded.

She admitted him almost immediately when he rang the bell outside her apartment door. He dropped his overnight bag on the floor and carefully placed the bottle of champagne he'd bought the night before on the hall table and turned to smile at her.

His smile vanished. Her eyes were red and her face looked pale. "Oh, honey. What's wrong? What's happened?" He put his arms around her. Holding her close, he breathed in her sweet scent. God, he loved this woman.

She clutched at him and he felt her trembling. He stroked his hands across her shoulders and over her back. "Honey. What's the matter? What's wrong?" She didn't respond and he pulled away. He cupped her face between his palms and stared down into her beautiful silver-gray eyes. He saw pure misery and pain in her gaze. "What is it, Jenn? What's wrong? Please. Tell me."

Tears welled in her eyes and rolled down her cheeks. "Rick. Oh, Rick, I...I thought you cared about me. I thought you meant it when you said you were my man."

His heart thumped. Oh, God! What had happened to make her doubt him, just as he was beginning to think he might finally be winning her confidence? "I do...I did...I am yours, Jennifer. I have been almost since our first date."

She pulled back and he reluctantly dropped his hands from her face. She brushed at her wet cheeks with the backs of her hands and lifted her chin. "Oh, really? Where were you last night?"

"Where was I last night? I told you were I was going to be. I was working...why?" He remembered suddenly that he had turned his phone and pager off. "Did you want me? Did you need me?"

"Working? Is that what you're standing there telling me? That you were working last night?"

"Yes. That's exactly what I'm standing here telling you. Jenn, let's not play games. If you have a problem, spit it out."

She tossed her head angrily. "I'm not the one with the problem, Rick! If you'll just be honest with me, we can get past this. Just admit where you were and what you were doing. It won't be easy to accept, but we can get past this because I...I want to be with you, Rick."

"I want to be with you...more than I've ever wanted to be with any other woman. You should know that by now...you must know that by now. What's wrong? What do you think I've done?"

She balled a hand into a fist and shook it at him. "It's not what I think...it's what I know. How long have you been seeing her, Rick?"

"How long have I been...how long have I been seeing who? I'm not seeing anyone other than you. You know that."

"No, no, I don't know that. I thought I did, but I don't. In fact, I know just the opposite."

He raked a hand through his hair and told himself not to panic. There was some misunderstanding between them, but they could and would work through it. "Okay. What exactly is it that you think you know? Tell me and we'll see what's going on here, Jenn."

"I know you weren't working at your office last night like you told me you were going to be," she spit the accusation out, her silver eyes blazing with a combination of pain and anger.

He wanted so much to take her in his arms and reassure her that he loved her, but there was a definite 'touch me not' aura surrounding her.

"Why did you lie to me? Why did you tell me you were going to be at your office working when you weren't?"

Okay, so she'd obviously called the office and was upset when he didn't answer. "Jenn, I never said I would be working at the office. "

"How can you stand there and say that?"

"I can say it because it's true. I told you I'd be working late—I didn't say where."

"Okay, you didn't say where. Do you put in all your overtime in a hotel bedroom?"

"A hotel bedroom? What are you talking about? I wasn't in any hotel..." he broke off abruptly and stared at her. She had somehow learned that he'd been at the hotel the night before. How was he going to convince her that he'd been in a restaurant and had never been anywhere near one of the rooms? "Why all these questions about last night? What's the matter?"

"I'll tell you what's the matter. All I want from you was the truth. Just tell me why and we can get past this because I want you, Rick. Just tell me why you were with her."

"Why I was with who?" he snapped angrily. "I told you the truth. I was working. I was not in any damned hotel room with anyone else. I don't know who's been trying to cause trouble between us, Jenn, but I was not with another woman!"

"I saw the two of you outside the hotel — kissing each other. So don't you dare stand there, telling me you were working and you belong to me only. I saw you with that slender redhead. You couldn't keep your hands off her until you got home. I mean, you'd obviously been in the hotel making love and yet there you were right in front of the hotel kissing like that!"

He sucked in a deep breath. Oh, God! Damn Connie Betton. Jennifer had somehow seen Connie spring that unwanted kiss on him and misunderstood. Still, he only had to explain and they would laugh about her jumping to the wrong conclusion. "Oh, Jenn! Honey, you misunderstood. We were at the hotel, but we were in the restaurant and I was working. We were both working overtime."

"You were kissing her."

"I did not kiss her. She kissed me."

"Big difference!"

He sighed and kept a tight rein on his temper. "Let me explain what happened. We'd just finished a deal and she'd just told me Hunter and Markham was the successful bidder on this contract we've been trying to land for months. Outside the hotel, we were saying goodbye and out of nowhere, she threw her arms around my neck and kissed me. If you were watching, then you must have seen that I not only did not kiss her back, but I also immediately pulled away from her."

To his amazement, she shook her head. "Oh, I was watching all right, Rick. I saw it all with my own eyes. You kissed her. Granted it wasn't a long kiss, but you definitely kissed her.

When she walked away from you, you went tearing after her like a little greedy puppy that couldn't wait for another helping.

"Tell me, Rick, did you tell her she intoxicated you and you couldn't give up fucking her unprotected pussy too?! Did you feed her the spiel about being the only woman you wanted?"

He closed his eyes briefly and took a deep, calming breath. Her lack of faith in him bit into him like the sting of an angrily wielded wet whip. Still, they could get past it if she'd only give him the benefit of the doubt.

"Jennifer, I just told you what happened. We were both working late in one of the hotel restaurants. We were never in any of the hotel rooms. I have never kissed or fucked her or even wanted to. Hell, I'm not even attracted to her. I will admit that she appears to be attracted to me, but nothing happened other than that brief kiss you saw outside in front of the hotel. And I did not kiss her back."

"Then why did you go home with her?"

"I didn't go home with her!"

"You followed her."

"To her car to ensure she reached it safely. Jennifer, I don't believe this crap...no, this shit! Everything I said about how I feel about you and what I wanted from a relationship with you was true. How the hell can you think I want some skinny, flat-chest redhead after having been your lover?"

"You want to know what I think, Rick? I think you want to have your damned cake and to eat it too! Well, you can't have both. If you want to see and fuck other women, fine. You shouldn't have lied to me and let me think you felt something for me you clearly don't."

"You have no idea what I feel...about anything, Jennifer. I have not lied to you. I never touched her. I never wanted to touch her. Once I'd slept with you, I never wanted to touch any other woman, but I guess I didn't understand just how little you trusted me. I don't understand what's up with you. You surrender your body…you allow me to make unprotected love to you, but you refuse to extend an ounce of faith my way.

"How can you believe, after all these weeks we've been lovers, that I want another woman? What did I do or say to deserve your lack of trust? How the hell can you possibly believe that I was fucking her or any other woman?"

"I know what I saw," she whispered, her voice trembling.

"You didn't see shit! How the hell can you have so little faith in me? What have these last few months been about? Has this all just been physical for you, Jennifer? You don't care shit about me. Do you? You never have and you never will. We never really got pass your stupid shit about not being able to trust a man with blond hair, have we?

"Well, you know what? If that's where you are, fine. I can't do anything about that. I thought we had something worthwhile together, but now I see I've just been a man with a big dick for you. But you know what? I'm too old for this shit. I want a woman who's ready to marry me and have my babies. I need a woman, who above all, will love and trust me. I told you what happened, but you think what the fuck you like."

He sucked in a deep, angry breath. "This whole thing with you has been one big, damn mistake. You go get yourself a man with black or brown or green hair that you can love and trust." He snatched up his overnight case from the floor. "As for me, I'm going to go find myself a slender, fucking blonde who trusts me."

He half hoped she would relent and beg him not to go. He needed her to tell him she was sorry and that she loved and trusted him. Hell, she wouldn't even have to apologize. If she just told him she loved him, he would stay and work on gaining her trust. But she let him go without a word of protest.

In his car, he sat with his head back against the rest, his heart thumping so hard he found breathing difficult. He was too damn old to cry. Besides, real men don't cry, but he felt as if his heart had been crushed and there was no air in his lungs. He was suffocating. How could this be happening? He was in love for the first time in his life. How could she not share his feelings? What was he supposed to do without her in his life? How was he ever going to get over her?

Chapter Twelve

"You need to give her another chance, Rick."

"No!" He sprang to his feet from the kitchen table where he and Angie were sitting over uneaten sandwiches. He stormed down the length of the kitchen before turning back to face her. "She called me a liar more times than I can remember. Then she accused me of cheating on her — when the thought of cheating on her, never...never entered my head. After our first date, she became unforgettable for me. The more I saw her, the harder I fell for her."

She stretched out a hand to him and he clutched it between both of his. She looked up at him. "Rick, a woman..." she paused and sighed. "A full-figured woman in love with a big, handsome man is sometimes just a little more vulnerable than one of the slender blondes you were so fond of would be. She probably only half believed that you really wanted her...just the way she was with no need for her to lose weight or change herself in anyway."

"I never gave her any reason to doubt me. None! I couldn't wish for her to be a single ounce lighter. I love everything about her...everything. I love that she feels heavy and warm in my arms when we make love. I love that she doesn't peck at her food. I love the way she seems to be comfortable with her weight...I love the color of her eyes...the length and thickness of her hair...I love the sound of her laugh...the way she looks when she wakes in the morning...there isn't anything about her that I don't absolutely adore. I love her."

"Did you tell her?"

"That I love her? No."

"Why not?"

"I knew she wasn't ready to hear it."

"How did you know that if you didn't tell her?"

"I just knew…"

"I think you should have told her. If she'd known you loved her, maybe she wouldn't have been so quick to think the wrong thing." She lifted his hands to her mouth and kissed them. "I know you are hurting, Rick and I hurt for you and with you, but I really think you should consider giving her another chance."

He shook his head. "If I did and we tried again, what kind of relationship would we have when she obviously doesn't trust me? She never has and never will."

"Never is a long time, Rick. Take a few days and think about whether or not you really want it to be over."

"Even if I wanted to give it another chance, she's not likely to still be interested. She's called several times, but…"

"You didn't talk to her."

"No. What was there to say?"

She shrugged. "You could tell her the truth: that you love her and want to try again."

"I don't know that I do want to try again. I don't know, Ange." He bent and kissed her cheek and gently pulled his hand away.

"Hey, can a man come into his own kitchen?"

They both looked up to see Troy standing in the doorway.

Angie looked at him with a questioning look in her eyes. He inclined his head slightly. She frowned and rose to her feet. "Hey, did I give you permission to leave your room?" she demanded.

Troy laughed and slipping behind her, he put his arms around her. "Sherri is sound asleep and I've been a good husband, so I thought maybe it would all right to leave without your permission just this once."

"Well...okay, as long as you don't make a habit of it." She leaned her head back against his shoulder.

Troy kissed the top of her head and looked at him. "Rick?"

He shook his head and shrugged. "I'm fine."

"Fine?"

"Okay, not exactly fine, but I'll be all right."

"Is there anything I can do to help? Anything at all?"

He shook his head. "She doesn't trust or love me. There's nothing anyone can do about that."

"Rick...man, I've never seen you so miserable. Are you sure you shouldn't try to work it out with her?"

"Yes! She's determined to make me atone for the sins of the men who hurt her, as if they're my sins."

"Rick...I know her lack of faith hurts like hell, but you're in love with her. What's the alternative to trying to work it out?"

"What's to work out? She thinks I'm a lying cheat! Look, I don't want to talk about her, Troy."

"Okay, but if you need either of us, Rick, we're always here for you."

"Always and any time," Angie said.

"I know and I can't tell either of you how much I appreciate that."

"Does it help a little?" she asked.

Nothing could help except having Jennifer back in his life. He smiled. "Of course it does, sweets," he lied.

He met Troy's gaze. He knew he wasn't deceiving Troy, but he didn't want Angie stressing out on his behalf.

Troy smiled slightly. "Are you up for some good news?"

He nodded. "If it's one thing I could use, it's good news."

Troy kissed Angie on the back of her neck. "Do you want to tell him or shall I?"

She looked at Rick, her dark eyes shinning. "I will." She extended a hand to him and he approached and took it in his. "Troy and I are—"

"Pregnant," Troy burst out, a wide smile lighting his face. "We're going to have another baby, man. Can you believe it?"

He smiled and hugged them both. "Oh, man, guys, that's great. Congratulations!" He stood back and looked at Angie. "And just how pregnant are we?"

"Three months," Troy said, stroking both hands over her stomach.

Looking at the two of them so happy and still in love with each other, he felt the loss of Jennifer even more acutely. This is what he had so desperately wanted to have with Jennifer. All he'd wanted was to be her man, husband, and someday the father of her children. Instead, he was going to have to learn to deal with the emptiness their breakup had caused in his life and heart. Somehow, he would have to forget her.

* * * * *

"Oh, Jenn, girl, I am so sorry." Cherica leaned down and wrapped her arms around her neck. "Are you sure it didn't happen like he said?"

"I saw them, Rica! I saw him kiss her!"

"But, Jenn, from what you told me, it could have happened just as he said. Maybe you were too hasty. Maybe you should give him another chance to explain before you just give him his walking papers."

She jerked away and walked across the living room floor to look out onto Cherica's balcony. "I was willing to listen to him, Rica. I just wanted him to admit what happened and promise me he wouldn't stray again. I knew it wouldn't be easy, but I love him and I would forget and forgive." She swung around to face Cherica. "But he refused to confess and then he said he didn't need this shit from me and that our whole relationship had been a big mistake."

"Jenn, I know this isn't easy for you, but try to see it from his point of view. If nothing happened, he had nothing to confess. If that's true, naturally he was angry and hurt that you didn't believe him. Just tossing him out of your life this way doesn't feel right."

"I didn't toss him out! He walked out! He said he was going to go find a slender blonde who trusted and loved him and he walked out on me!" She bit her lip to hold back the sobs making her throat ache.

"Okay. I'm sure you both said some hateful, hurtful things to each other, but nothing you can't forgive each other for, if you're in love. I think you should call him."

"Why should I be the one to call him?"

Cherica cast a brief gaze upward. "Because you're the one who accused him of infidelity. If he wasn't unfaithful, think how that must have hurt."

She turned away and stared out the balcony doors. She'd thought of very little else during the last two weeks. Maybe she shouldn't have been so quick to think badly of him. Why hadn't she heard him out and then been willing to trust him when he insisted he hadn't kissed the woman? After all, the kiss had been very brief and he had made no attempt to touch the woman when he'd followed her.

She recalled that whenever they were together, he couldn't keep his hands off of her. When they were alone, he liked to fondle her ass and her breasts endlessly. In public, he either kept an arm around her shoulders or held her held. He had done neither with the redhead. He very well could have had nothing to confess…and she'd accused him of being unfaithful repeatedly and so very harshly while disdainfully dismissing his attempts to explain. No wonder he considered their time together a big mistake.

She hugged her arms around her body and closed her eyes. "Rica, I guess I'm afraid that he really was telling the truth and now he doesn't want anything to do with me."

Cherica approached her and pressed her cheek against her back. "I don't know if I'd be so quick to believe that, if I were you, Jenn. He was hurt and he probably said what he thought would hurt you most. I think you should call him and discuss it."

She sighed. "I've tried. I've called him ten times in the last nine days. When I call him at home, I get his answering machine. I leave messages, but he never returns my calls. When I call him at work, I can't get past his secretary, who keeps telling me he's unavailable, but she'll take a message."

Cherica patted her on the back and moved away. "Okay. Jenn, I don't know about you, but I think maybe you owe him an apology."

"I know that! I do, but he won't let me give him one. I don't even know anymore what I saw. Two weeks ago, it seemed so clear what was happening. Now I'm just about convinced that he was telling the truth."

"If he won't talk to you on the phone, take him on in person. Go to his office and force him to see you."

"I can't do that."

"Why not?"

"What if he won't see me? Think how humiliating that would be."

"Jenn, you need to get your priorities straight. Isn't the possibility of winning back the man you love worth a little humiliation? You know what? I'll bet he's just as in love with you as you are with him."

She turned to look at Cherica. "Do you think so?"

"Jenn, have you ever seen the way he looks at you? As if you're the only woman in the world. I'm telling you. You have to make an effort to win him back. I know it won't be easy, but I'll bet he's worth it."

The harsh reality was that she wanted him back—even if she had to humiliate herself in the process.

* * * * *

After several more sleepless nights, Jennifer decided to do as Cherica suggested and try to force a meeting at Rick's office. As she dressed, she left her hair down on her shoulders, the way Rick preferred. She felt gauche and afraid walking into his office. She smiled at the receptionist. "Good morning. My name is Jennifer Rose. Is…is Mr. Markham in? I'd like to see him."

"Ah…"

She swallowed quickly. The shuttered look on the receptionist's face made it fairly clear this was the woman who had been taking her messages for over two weeks.

"Ah, have a seat please and I'll check to see if…he's available."

Feeling her cheeks burning, she turned and sat in one of the chairs along one wall on the opposite side of the room. She watched the receptionist pick up the phone. There was a brief, soft voiced conversation. Her whole body felt as if it were on fire. He was going to humiliate her by refusing to see her. She was a fool for coming.

She rose, deciding that she wouldn't give him the satisfaction.

The receptionist put the phone down and looked at her in surprise. "He'll be out shortly."

"Oh. Thank you." Before she could sink back into the chair, Rick appeared in the doorway to the right of the receptionist's desk.

Her heart thumped and her throat felt tight as he walked towards her. "Jennifer. We can talk in my office. This way." He nodded at the receptionist. "I don't want to be disturbed. Thank you."

She followed him down a short hallway and into the office at the end. He opened the door and stepped aside. She preceded him inside. He followed her and closed the door. "Have a seat."

"I'd rather stand."

He leaned back against the door. "What can I do for you?"

She stared at him. She could detect no tenderness or warmth in him. Could this be the same man who had made such sweet, passionate love to her? Was this the same man who couldn't get enough of holding her hand, fondling her breasts and rear end, or just having her sit on his lap?

She licked her lips. "Rick, we need to talk."

He shook his head. "There's nothing left to say. You don't trust me and I am not going to be involved in a relationship with a woman who doesn't trust me. I told you the truth and you called me a liar sixteen different ways from Sunday. There's nothing left to talk about."

"I...I was talking to Cherica and I realized that maybe I...did misunderstand what I saw. "

His eyes narrowed. "So? That's supposed to make me feel better? You had to hear it from your friend before you were willing to admit you *might* have misunderstood? My word wasn't good enough. You were so ready to mistrust me that you jumped to the wrong conclusion and refused to believe the truth even when it was told to you. You know what, Jennifer? I don't need or want that kind of a relationship. I'm at a point in my life when I want to be married to a woman who loves and trust me implicitly. And that sure the hell ain't you, Jennifer."

You are not going to cry. She bit her lip and fought off a sense of panic. The cold, angry look in his blue-green eyes assured her that no matter what she said or did, he was finished with her. He'd probably never really cared for her. She swallowed a lump of pain and despair before lifting her chin. Abandoning her pride wasn't going to accomplish anything.

"Fine, Rick...if that's the way you feel...I was a fool for coming here. But I just...okay, I can accept that you never loved or cared about me as a person and you don't want to see me anymore...I finally get the message. I won't bother you again. I know it doesn't matter to you, but it matters to me...please tell me...did you make love to her?"

"Hell no!" He stormed over to her and gripped her shoulders. "How many times can I tell you that I didn't fuck her? I never wanted to touch her. You were the center of my world, Jennifer. You. I didn't want or need any other woman. I was in love with you. I was spitting close to asking you to marry me. What made you think I wanted her or any other woman? When we were together, how could you not know how I felt about you? No matter what you say, I know now I never stood a real chance with you. I can't deal with you on any other level. If that's clear, I'm rather busy."

He released her and walked across the room to open the door.

Despite her best efforts, tears welled in her eyes and spilled down her cheeks. "Rick..."

"Jennifer, please. It's over. There's no need to cry...there was never much between us worth crying over. I don't want to talk to you. I don't want to see you. I just want to forget you and move on with my life. Just leave me alone and I'll leave you alone. Please."

She put a hand over her face. "Oh, God!" It couldn't end like this. She wanted and needed him too much.

He swore softly and then she heard the door open and close.

She dropped her hand and realized she was alone in the room. She knew she needed to leave, but she just couldn't. The sofa against the wall seemed to beckon her. She sank onto it and let her tears flow, sucking in deep, gulping breaths. *Oh, God, oh, God, oh, God!* Please. She wasn't going to be forgiven for the awful mistake she'd made. What kind of love was it that wouldn't allow him to forgive her? How could he not understand how it had looked from her point of view? Why couldn't he give her another chance?

She gave an angry shake of her head. Enough whining and feeling sorry for herself. He had left her alone to give her time to regain her composure. She opened her cosmetic bag and redid her makeup. *Now go and do not look back.*

Halfway across the room, the office door opened and Rick came back in. He closed the door and leaned against it. "Are you going to be okay to drive? If you like, I can have one of our interns drive you home."

"No. I don't need...I'll be fine. I'm leaving now. And don't worry. You won't ever see or hear from me again."

He sighed. "Look. That might have been a little harsh, Jennifer. I'm sorry it had to end like this. I never wanted it to end like this. Hell, I never wanted it to end at all." He stepped away from the door. "Are you sure you don't need someone to drive you home?"

"I'm positive."

"Would you do me a favor? When you get home, will you call my secretary and let her know you got home? Just so I'll know you arrived safely?"

She nodded. "Ah...goodbye." She reached for the doorknob.

He put a hand against the panel to keep the door closed. "Jennifer...I know I said I didn't want to see you or talk to you again..."

Was he having second thoughts? She could barely breath.

"And I meant it," he went on, crushing the last vestige of hope in her. "But of course if you're pregnant, that would change everything. If you are, you'll tell me. Won't you? I meant what I said about standing by you. I will be there for you and the baby. You understand that, don't you?"

It would be a cold day in hell before she ever subjected herself to being hurt by him again. Still, she nodded silently, not looking at him.

"Jennifer...I'm sorry you think I was unfaithful and I'm sorry you're hurt. I never wanted to do anything to hurt you. I miss you and..." He opened the door. "Goodbye."

Fresh tears filled her eyes. All the other hurts in her past paled in comparison to the despair and anguish she felt now. Having her heart torn out could hurt no worse. It couldn't end like this without so much as a kiss. It wasn't going to end like this. It was over, but she wanted something to remember their good times by.

She closed the door and looked at him. "Rick...I don't suppose you'd like..."

"You don't suppose I'd like what?"

"One final, farewell fuck. A quickie...right here...right now."

He stared down at her and she saw the indecision in his eyes. Finally, he gave a slight shake of his head.

"Are you sure?" She leaned against the door and meeting his gaze, she lifted her skirt, exposing her bare mound.

When he didn't react, she bit her lip, sucked in a deep breath, and spoke in a rush. "What about some ass? Would you like a piece of ass before we part?"

"Ass? You mean..."

"I mean would you like to fuck my ass with something other than your finger...like your cock."

"You don't mean that."

"I do."

He shook his head again, but reached out a hand to touch her. She shivered and closed her eyes. He palmed her mound and flicked his thumb against her clit. She bit her lip and parted her legs.

She heard his zip and the tearing of a foil package. She opened her eyes and looked up at him. The look in his eyes, cold and lustful, made her heart ache. It also filled her with apprehension. She knew he was going to fuck her to hurt her. He wasn't going to make any concession for the fact that she'd never had a cock shoved up her behind.

He turned her around. He moved behind her and she felt him parting her cheeks with one hand while he held his cock in his other. She closed her eyes, tensed her body, and waited for the pain. No matter how much it hurt, she promised herself that she would not cry out or shed a single tear.

He pinched her ass cheeks, bit her neck, and shoved against her. Her eyes flew open. Surely, he didn't mean to take her without any foreplay or lube. He hadn't so much as kissed or caressed her or done anything to arouse her.

She felt his cock sliding between her cheeks and pressed her cheek against her door, waiting for the pain. He suddenly jerked away from her, spun her around, pushed her back against the door, and urged her legs apart. Then without a word, he pushed roughly against her and she gasped as he slammed his cock balls deep into her with one angry movement. But thank God it slid into her pussy and not her ass.

He took her against the door. He gripped her hips tightly as he fucked her without the least ounce of tenderness. She kept her eyes closed on the tears welling in them. Even on their first night as lovers, he'd shown her more tenderness and consideration than he did now. There was no fondling or kissing, just hard, almost angry plunges into her pussy, making her behind jiggle against the door panel. He came well before she was even close to climaxing.

He stood with his body pressed against her, his cock still imbedded deep in her aching, unfulfilled pussy. This wasn't how she'd wanted or expected their last time together to be. She shoved against his shoulders.

He lifted his head and looked down at her. His eyes were dark with passion and desire. "You didn't enjoy that."

"No, I didn't!" she snapped, "but then you didn't intend me to enjoy it, did you?"

His eyes narrowed. "Why play the martyr? It was your idea to have a quickie."

"I didn't ask you to practically rape me!"

"It wasn't rape!" he snapped. "And you damn well know it wasn't."

"Maybe not," she allowed, "but I feel like I've just been treated like a piece of shit by you! You made no allowances or concessions for my feelings or needs. Just stabbed your cock in me, pounded my pussy like it was a piece of meat, shot off your rocks, and to hell with me."

A hint of red touched his cheeks. "Isn't that what you meant by a quickie?"

"No and you damn well know it! Why would I want to be treated like that by a man who claimed he was once in love with me?" She shoved at his shoulders again. "I'd better go before I start to hate you."

"I wish I could hate you."

"I want to leave, Rick."

He curled his hands in her hair and pressed his forehead against hers. "Damn! Damn! I'm sorry." He pulled out of her, but kept his body against hers. "I'm sorry, Jenn." He laced his fingers through hers. "That's not how I want our last time together to be."

"Then why you'd you do it?"

"It could have been worse," he pointed out. "I could have taken the ass you so graciously offered."

She flushed and longed to slap his face until her palms stung. "Why didn't you? From the way you ripped into my pussy, I'm sure you would have loved tearing into my ass."

"Don't flatter yourself, Jennifer. If I really want a piece of ass, I don't have to settle for yours."

That was the absolute last thing she expected him to say. It was also the most painful. Her eyes filled with tears and she sucked in a gasping breath. "You bastard!"

"Shit!" He slammed a fist against the door panel by her head. "I didn't mean that!" He curled his fingers in her hair and forced her to look at him. "I did not mean that. God, I didn't mean it! Don't cry! I didn't mean it! I just said it to hurt you, but I didn't mean it."

The tears spilled down her cheeks and she stared at him, unable to speak pass the hurt in her chest.

He gathered her in his arms and rocked her against him. "Please. Don't cry. There's no need. I didn't mean it. I'm so sorry." He kissed her hair and cupped her face between his palms. "Let me make it up to you."

She shook her head, the tears still streaming down her cheeks.

He rubbed his semi hard cock along the length of her pussy. "I'm still hard." He pressed the head of his cock between her cunt lips. Despite herself, she trembled. "And you're still moist. I have a hard cock and you have a hot, moist pussy. I'll make it up to you, Jenn. I promise."

"What? I should let you hammer my pussy again with no regard for my pleasure? Hell no, Rick!"

"That was a big mistake and I am so sorry. That won't ever happen again." He pressed forward, allowing a several inches of his cock to pierce her pussy. "Let me make it up to you."

Her pussy was itching and burning with smoldering embers of lust. Pure and simple, she wanted and needed his cock in her pussy.

She knew she was being weak, but she made no protest as he led her over to the sofa.

She kept her eyes closed and he quickly undressed her and urged her onto her back. He knelt beside the sofa and stroked one hand over her body as the fingers of his other hand found their way into her cunt. He finger fucked her and gently sucked at her breasts, all the while whispering to her that he was sorry he'd hurt her.

Lord, she loved the way he allowed the tip of his tongue to circle her hardening nipples before greedily gobbling her breasts into his mouth. Liquid heat and white passion engulfed her. Moisture pooled between her legs. Passion flicked at her senses.

She bit her lip to silence her moans and felt her hips jerking wildly against his hand.

Her pussy ached to be invaded by his big, thick cock again. "Oh, please," she begged. "Please."

He whispered to her softly as he lay on top of her and began kissing her. He then filled her pussy with cock with one quick thrust that made her toes curl. "Ahhh!"

"Oh, damn, your pussy is exquisite," he groaned. "It fits around my cock like a tight, moist vice. Oh, shit. This is good!" Rolling them over so they were on their sides with her behind against the back of the sofa, he surprised and dismayed her by pulling his cock out of her. He pressed against her, his thumb flicking at her clit.

She was swept up in a sensual whirlpool, her senses battered by wild currents of lust and desire. He caressed and stroked her until every fiber of her body burned and ached for him. "Please...oh, please."

"Oh, yeah, baby. I'm coming." He settled his body against hers and positioned himself at her entrance.

"Now. Please."

He lapped at her breasts. "Yes. Now, baby. Now."

When she felt his cock begin the slow, delicious slid into her pussy, she sobbed softly and clutched at him. Halfway inside her, he paused and kissed her gently.

As she returned the sweet pressure of his mouth, he propelled the rest of his shaft into her. Kissing her tears away, he began a gentle but hungry fuck rhythm inside her. He repeatedly withdrew nearly his entire rod, only to plunge it back into her cunt. He frequently stopped fucking her to lay against her, suck her breasts, and flick her clit, sending endless charges of electric delight out from her pussy and through her entire body. Finally, she had to bite into his shoulder to keep from crying out when she exploded around his pummeling cock.

Pressing her tight against the sofa back, he lifted one of her legs over his thigh and thrust into her with a heated force and vigor which ignited a new fire in her already burning cunt. She clung to him, overcome with lust and need, her pussy greedily convulsing around his shaft.

Finding his mouth, she devoured his sweet lips and met him thrust for thrust, joyfully receiving the hot cock ramming in and out of her pussy. She lingered on the edge of the cliff of satisfaction as yet another climax threatened to overtake her. When he groaned and began stabbing his dick into her in a frenzy, he drove them both over the edge and down the side of the mountain of desire and straight into the valley of pure bliss. Lord, what a lovely, lovely feeling.

They lay on the sofa, still joined for several minutes after they'd both come. He kissed her lips gently and stroked her shoulders and back, soothing her. As he'd become accustomed to doing, he dipped a finger in her pussy to lube it, then he gently inserted it up her ass.

Lord, his finger felt good up there, poking and stroking her nether regions. She trembled and longed to tell him how sorry she was and how much she wanted another chance with him. But she knew that nothing had changed between them. Finally, he kissed her lips and pulled out of her pussy and her ass. He discarded the condom and surprised her by urging her onto her back and lying on top of her.

He stroked her cheeks. "I hope that helps to make up for before," he told her.

It didn't really, but what was the point in saying so?

She turned her head and kissed his palm.

Their gazes met and just for a moment, she thought he would soften towards her, but he sighed and rolled away.

An hour later, she was home in the shower with cool water pouring over her. Although her heart ached, she didn't cry. It was over between them. No amount of tears could change that.

Chapter Thirteen

"Julie and I are going out to Club Ruben this weekend. Why don't you come with?"

Jennifer looked across the few feet that separated her and Cherica on the track. Still swinging her arms and walking briskly, she shook her head. "I think I'll pass."

"Oh, come on, Jenn. It might just be what you need. You can't continue to sit home eating your heart out over him. If he's so unforgiving, maybe you're better off without him."

Maybe so, but she didn't want to go out looking for another relationship or even casual sex until her heart didn't feel so damned bruised. That was going to take time. Her need for him was still the driving force in her life. Three weeks later, she still fell asleep thinking of the last time they'd made love in his office. If what had happened could be called making love.

"Rica, I just don't feel like clubbing."

"But you have to start trying to forget him, Jenn and where better to do it than in a club with men who like their women large and voluptuous?"

"I'm having mom and Paul over for dinner on Friday."

"Really?"

Cherica sounded surprised and she nodded.

"Ladies, we're about to pick up the pace," the instructor called out.

"Yes. I think I was wrong about him. He's not after mom's money. He made a killing in real estate and retired two years ago. He has condos all over the place and is always buying her expensive gifts. I misjudged him…just as I did Rick."

"Later for Rick," Cherica muttered. "Who the hell is he to hurt you like this?"

She shrugged. "I want to make amends to Mom and Paul for the way I behaved. He seems to be a really nice guy and he makes her so happy. It's the least I can do."

"I'm glad you've come to terms with your mom and her guy," Cherica said. "So Friday is out. What about Saturday or Sunday?"

She shook her head. "Rica, I know you and Julie are worried about me and I appreciate that, but I'm just not ready to go out yet. Give me a few more weeks and I'll be all right."

"Jenn, you're not pregnant, are you?"

Cherica sounded alarmed and she smiled slightly. "No." The last time in his office, Rick had used condoms. She wished now that he hadn't. She would have liked to experience the joy of feeling his baby growing inside her.

"Okay, ladies. Pick up the pace on three," the instructor called out. "One…two…double-time. Long strides and swinging arms for this last half mile, ladies."

"I'm be all right," she assured Cherica. "Really."

And she would. She hurt, but she would get over Rick.

* * * * *

She got up early the next morning and spent the day cleaning and cooking, preparing for dinner that night. She kept the music on her stereo upbeat and didn't allow her thoughts to dwell on Rick. By the time her mother and Paul arrived, she was feeling the strain of trying not to think about Rick.

They were holding hands and looking like the perfect couple when she opened her apartment door. She experienced an unwanted jealousy that shamed and depressed her. Now she was reduced to begrudging her own mother her much-deserved happiness.

She forced a smiled. "Mom. Paul. It's great to see you both. Come in and take a load off." She kissed her mother's cheek. A nice warmth spread through her when Paul bent and kissed her cheek.

"Thanks for having me over, Jennifer."

Her smile became a genuine one. She gave his hand a squeeze. "Thanks for coming." She decided that just maybe the evening wasn't going to be such a chore after all.

Over dinner on the balcony, they laughed and talked sports. At least, she and Paul talked sports. Her mother sat with a wide smile on her face, alternatively staring at them in turn. Jennifer knew she was pleased that they were getting along so well.

After dinner, she cleared the table and went into the kitchen to get the iced tea from the refrigerator. She filled the ice bucket, put the clean glasses on a tray, and headed back onto the balcony.

She stopped abruptly at the door and stared onto the balcony. Her mother was in Paul's arms and he was pressing long, hot kisses against her lips, while he stroked his hands over her behind.

The tray slipped from her fingers and she turned and ran back through the apartment and into her bedroom. She fell across the bed and tears ran down her cheeks.

"Jennifer?"

She heard her mother's voice in her bedroom door and turned her face into her pillow.

"Oh, Jennifer. Darling, I'm so sorry." Her mother sat on the side of the bed and stroked her hair and shoulders as she used to do when Jennifer was very young. "Darling, we didn't mean to offend you. I know you're still finding it hard to accept your father's untimely death and…"

"It's not that anymore, Mom," she whispered.

"Then what is it, love?" Her mother stretched out on the bed beside her and put an arm around her. "What is it, love?"

She told her about Rick.

"Oh, my poor, beautiful, darling." Her voice trembled and she kissed her hair. "What's his full name and where does he live and work? I won't have you hurt like this. I'll go to him and make him see reason, if I have to give him a good old-fashion shaking."

The thought of her small, petite mother giving Rick an old-fashion shaking was enough to force a small smile from her. She sat up and wiped at her cheeks. "Oh, Mom, I love you!"

"What's his name, Jennifer? I won't have him treat you this way."

"Mom, he has a legitimate complaint. I didn't trust him when I should have. He's not going to change his mind."

Her mother sat up, her dark eyes narrowing. "Then you'll just have to give him a reason to change his mind."

She shook her head. "I've already tried everything I know, including humiliating myself."

"Then try something else. Jennifer, true love doesn't come along for everyone. When you find the man that makes you complete in every way, you have to fight tooth and nail to keep him. I've been fortunate, it's happened to me twice in one lifetime. I want that same wonderful experience for you. If he's the one man you've been waiting for, Jennifer, you can't let him go without trying everything. If he really loved you as he said, he's probably looking for a reason to give your relationship another chance. Give him that reason, darling."

She put her head on her mother's shoulder. "I couldn't bear to have him reject me again, Mom. It hurts too much."

"What's his name and where does this sanctimonious man live? If you won't face him, then I will."

"Mom!" She sat up. "No! He meant what he said."

"So do I. Now what's his full name? Is Rick short for Richard? What's his last name?"

She shook her head. "Mom, I'm not telling you! It's over. The last time I saw him, he begged me not to contact him again and I promised I wouldn't."

"Well, I didn't and I will have my say, Jennifer." She rose. "If you won't tell me, I'll find out on my own who he is and when I do, he will have to answer to me."

"Mom! No! Please."

"Jennifer, I'll make it perfectly clear to him that you insisted I stay away from him, but he will be hearing from me."

She stared at her mother. She knew that look. Nothing she could say or do would change her mother's mind. "Please," she said again. "Don't."

"I have too, Jennifer. I can't bear to see you like this."

"I'll be all right," she said desperately. "Please don't contact him."

"You just leave this to me, darling." She extended her hand. "Now, can we go back onto the balcony and explain to Paul that you're no longer opposed to our relationship?"

She nodded. "Yes. I had no business being opposed to it in the first place. I'm sorry I made this so difficult for you, Mom."

She pressed her cheek against Jennifer's shoulder. "Never mind, love. As long as you accept us now, we'll be so grateful. Paul will be grateful. He doesn't have any family and he is so eager to have you like him."

"No family? None?"

"He was the only child of only children who are now dead."

"Well, he must have some aunts and uncles or a cousin or two. Someone."

"No one he's ever told me about."

"Oh, Mom, I'm sorry. I didn't know."

"No matter, darling. Paul and I will be fine. And so will you and your Rick."

She sighed and shrugged. She shouldn't have told her mother about Rick. Now she was going to make it her life's work to get her and Rick back together. Well, her mother wouldn't be able to confront Rick without knowing his last name or where he lived or worked.

On the other hand, maybe her mother had the right idea. Maybe she should try one more time to win him back. She savored the memory of his tenderness the last time they'd been together. Her mother didn't know where he was, but she did.

* * * * *

Rick came awake abruptly from yet another dream of Jennifer. He groaned and turned from his back onto his stomach. It had now been several weeks since he'd last seen her. When would the dreams and the need for her subside? He was beginning to think they wouldn't. His desire for her continued unabated. Maybe this was what real love was about. Maybe he couldn't forget her because deep down he didn't really want to forget her.

With her he had felt a sense of belonging and need he'd never expected to feel for anyone. He missed that and he missed her. Damn. He'd been a fool. He should have forgiven her. Wasn't that what love was all about? Besides, he'd never stopped to consider how that kiss must have looked from her point of view.

What would he have assumed in her place? Probably the same thing she had and he couldn't swear that he'd have been anymore willing to listen to reason than she'd been. Both Troy and Angie insisted that a big part of being in love was how vulnerable it made one feel. After all, hadn't he assumed that the man he'd seen with her at the club was her lover?

He was tired of missing her and tired of being miserable. He wanted and needed her and probably always would. It was time he did something about it. He turned and looked at his bedside clock. One-thirty a.m. It was too late to call her. Too late. Oh damn, he hoped he hadn't come to his senses too late.

He lay back against his pillow, his heart thumping with fear and anxiety. He had ignored her attempts to apologize and then made it worse by fucking her without the least consideration for her feelings and needs. She had made no attempt to contact him since she'd left his office that day.

She might no longer be interested in a relationship with a man that couldn't bend enough to forgive a mistake. Oh, shit! He buried his face in his pillow. If he had blown it with her, there was only one way to find out. In the morning, he would call her and ask if they could try again.

The next morning, he found that his resolve and his courage had dissipated with the light of day. What if she told him to go to hell and refused to see him? What was he supposed to do then? The mere thought triggered a near panic. Oh, God, she had to forgive him. If he had to beg and completely abandon his pride, so be it. If he won her back, it would be well worth it.

He showered and decided to try to soften her up with roses. He pulled his credit card from his wallet just as the phone rang.

"Hello."

"Is this Richard Markham?" A female voice asked.

No one other than his mother or business contacts called him Richard. "Yes," he said, wondering what business contact was calling him on a Saturday morning. "And you are?"

"Helen Rose."

"Helen…Rose? Are you any relation to Jennifer?"

"I'm her mother."

"Her mother?" He swallowed a sudden lump of fear. Why would her mother call him? "Is she…is Jennifer…all right?"

"No, she is not!"

He sucked in a breath and sank down onto the side of his bed. "How…how bad it is?"

"You actually sound as if you care."

"Oh, God, I do!" he whispered, feeling as if he couldn't breathe. "Please. How badly is she hurt?"

"We need to talk. I'm on my way to your house now. I should be there within the half hour."

He closed his eyes. Oh, God please. "Just tell me how badly she's hurt."

"When we meet. I want to look into the face of the man who hurt her so badly and tell you what I think of you," she said angrily and broke the connection.

He let the phone drop from his hand and fell back against the bed. He felt as if his lungs were crushed, making breathing almost impossible. *Okay, Rick,* he told himself. *You're jumping to conclusions. She is not dead. Do not freak out. When her mother arrives you'll find out how badly she's hurt and go from there.*

He got up and dressed. He made coffee and sat waiting for Helen Rose to arrive. An hour and a half later, he was still waiting.

He stopped pacing in his living room and decided he'd waited long enough. He called Jennifer's house. He got her answering machine. He waited half an hour, then called again. After the third call, he got in his car and drove to her apartment. In her building lobby, he stood staring at the names on the mailboxes, trying to remember her friend's name.

He thought her last name began with an N or M but he wasn't sure. Something like Mason. He spotted a B. Newton in apartment 2022. It didn't sound familiar, but he rang the bell.

"Yes?" A female answered.

"Ah, this is Rick. I was wondering if Jennifer is with you."

"You have the wrong apartment," the voice informed him and broke the connection.

Damn. He studied the names on the boxes again. There was a C. Martin in apartment 1820. He frowned. He was almost sure Jennifer's friend was named Sherry. He was used to Sherry being spelled with an S instead of a C, but people were spelling commonplace names differently these days. He pushed the buzzer. There was no response.

By the time he emerged from the lobby half an hour later, he was feeling desperate and more afraid than he'd ever been in his life. He called Troy and told him about the call from Jennifer's mother.

"Oh, man, Rick! Listen, Angie's spending the weekend with her parents. I have Sherri, but I'll take her to my parents then I'll be on my way to your house. Don't lose hope, Rick. I'm on my way."

Troy arrived just after he got home. Troy took one look at his face and embraced him.

He dropped his head against Troy's shoulder. "Oh, shit, Troy! I think I blew it! What if she's dead and I never accepted the apology she kept trying to give me and never told her I loved her."

Troy's arms tightened around him. "You don't know that she's dead or even how badly she's hurt, Rick." Troy tightened a fist in his hair and pushed him away. "The first thing we'll do is find out what hospital she's in. Where's the phone?"

He pointed to the arm of his recliner. He paced the length of the rec room. Despair, fear, and grief choked his ability to think clearly.

"And you're sure you haven't admitted a Jennifer Rose? I see. Thank you." Troy shook his head and put the phone down. "That's all of the city hospitals. We'll try the suburban ones next."

He raked a hand through his hair. "Maybe she's not there because she's already — "

Troy bounded to his feet and gripped his shoulders. "Rick, I know you're scared. Hell, man, I'm scared for you, but we don't know yet what's going on. Let's not put her in the morgue just yet. Okay?"

"Then where the hell is she, Troy?"

"I don't know, but we'll find out, Rick."

The ringing of the phone startled them both. He glanced at Troy. "You didn't tell Angie, did you?"

"Not yet, but I'll have to soon, Rick. She'll barbecue us both if we don't."

He moved across the room and picked up the phone. "Hello?"

"Rick! Oh, thank God you're there."

His knees buckled and he sank down to the floor, clutching the phone to his ear. "Oh, God! Jennifer!" He gulped in several deep breaths, barely aware of Troy sinking down to the floor next to him. "Jennifer! Oh, God, honey, where are you?"

"I'm at the hospital," she sobbed. "There's been an awful accident. Can you come?"

"At the hospital?" He closed his eyes and leaned his head against Troy's shoulder. *Oh, God, thank you,* he whispered softly. *Thank you, so much.* She was hurt, but she was alive, conscious, and wanting him with her.

"Can you come, Rick?"

"Yes!" He attempted to rise, but his legs refused to cooperate until Troy rose and pulled him to his feet. "Where are you, honey?"

She gave him the name of one of the hospitals Troy had called. "Hurry, Rick. Please."

"I'm on my way, Jennifer." He hung up and turned to look at Troy, his eyes filling with tears. "Troy! She's hurt, but she's alive man!"

"Oh, damn what a relief!" Troy wiped at a tear that had trickled down his cheek. They embraced briefly before pulling back. Troy chuffed his head. "I told you she wasn't dead!" They grinned at each other. "Okay. Let's get on the road. Where is she? I'll drive," Troy said.

Troy got them to the hospital within twenty minutes. Rick jumped out of the car as soon as it stopped. He ran across the parking lot and into the hospital.

"I'm here to see Jennifer Rose," he told the guard.

"How is the last name spelled?"

"R-O-S-E," he said and watched the guard check the commuter.

"When was she brought in?"

"I don't know. She called me from here less than a half an hour ago."

The guard shook her head. "There's no Jennifer Rose. Does she use another name?"

"No! She's here!"

"Not according to our records."

He leaned across the desk. "Then your records are wrong! She called me from here!"

"Rick?"

He swung around and saw Jennifer coming though a pair of glass doors behind the guard's desk. Although she had clearly been crying, he could see no signs of outward injuries. Another set of glass doors opened as she approached. She ran forward and burrowed into his arms. "Oh, Rick!"

"Oh, Jenny, honey. Honey." He clutched her to him and buried his face against her hair. "Oh, God, I thought I'd lost you." He kissed her hair and stared down into her red eyes. "What are you doing here? Are you all right? When your mother called me this morning and — "

"My mother called you?"

"Yes. Her name is Helen Rose. Isn't it?"

"Yes."

"When she called and said you were hurt, I thought…oh, God, I thought you were dead!"

"You thought I was dead? But I wasn't involved in the accident, Rick."

"Rick? Is everything okay?"

Troy stopped several feet from them. Keeping an arm around Jennifer, he beckoned Troy closer. "Jennifer, this is my best friend, Troy Hunter. Troy, this is Jennifer Rose."

To his surprise, Troy pulled Jennifer away from him and into his arms. "Oh, man, I am so glad to see you alive and well." He kissed her cheek. "In case he blows another chance to tell you, I think you should know that Rick has been miserable since you two stopped seeing each other and he's big time in love with you."

Troy kissed her cheek again and looked at him. "I'm going to go find the café and call Angie. Come find me when you're ready."

He watched Troy walk away before he turned to find Jennifer staring up at him, her eyes wide. "Did you hear what he…he said about you?"

He nodded. "Yes."

She licked her lips. "Is it…true?"

"Yes."

Her lips trembled and she turned into his arms. "Why didn't you tell me?"

"I should have, but I knew you didn't share my feelings."

She lifted her head and looked up at him. "Yes, I do, Rick. You have no idea how much I do."

He swallowed several times. "You…do?"

She nodded rapidly. "Yes! But we'll have to talk about that later. Right now I'm worried about my mother."

"Your mother? She never showed up after she called me this morning…was she in the accident?"

"Yes." Tears filled her eyes. "The car she and her friend were in was involved in a head-on collision." She clenched her fist in his shirt. "They're hurt really bad, Rick."

"Oh, honey." He kissed her hair.

"They're about to move my mother to a bed in ICU." She looked at the guard. "Would you buzz us back in, please?"

The guard nodded and pressed a button under her desk. Rick followed Jennifer through the emergency department. She stopped at the last room at the end of a corridor.

It contained several beds. She glanced briefly at the bed where an unconscious man with dark hair and a neck brace lay before moving on to the last bed in the room. The moment Rick saw the small, dark woman he knew she was Jennifer's mother. He could see that even though her face was bruised and swollen. She had a tube down her throat.

Jennifer touched her arm and whimpered. He moved behind her and put his arms around her. He didn't know what to say, so he just held her, hoping his presence provided her some measure of comfort.

Several people came up to the bed. "Ms. Rose, we are about to move your mother to her room now. If you two could just step outside the for a few moments while we get her ready to move?"

"Ah...can we come too?"

"Yes. You can follow. She's being taken to room 6020 in the Tutlemen Building."

She nodded and glanced at the man in the bed to their right. "And Mr. Westerfield? Is he also going to be moved to a room?"

"Yes, as soon as he's stabilized. You're sure he doesn't have any family?"

"None that I know of. I'll be in my mother's room. You'll let me know if there's anything I can do to help him?"

"We'll take the best care of him we can, Ms. Rose."

She turned and looked up at him with tears in her eyes. "If anything happens to him, my mother will be heartbroken."

"Your mother..." He glanced back at the man. "Is he the man you told me about?"

"Yes." She lifted her chin. "What about it?"

He shook his head. "I was just thinking how lucky he is."

"She's lucky too. He's a really great guy...like you. Thank you for coming when I needed you."

"I'll always come when you need me, Jennifer."

With tears spilling down her cheeks, she burrowed in his arms.

Chapter Fourteen

"Hey. Wake up, sleepy head."

Jennifer opened her eyes. She was sitting in one of the two chairs in her mother's hospital room. She glanced out the window and then at her watch. It was now light again. She straightened abruptly and glanced at the bed. Her eyes filled with tears as she saw her mother's eyelids fluttering.

The tube had been removed from her throat the day before and with some of the swelling of her face receding, she looked more like herself.

Rick, seated beside her smiled encouragement at her. "She's waking up." He rose. "I'll leave you alone."

"No." She took his hand and urged him to his feet. Still holding his hand, she approached the bed and touched her mother's face with her free hand. "Mom…?"

Helen Rose's eyes opened. A weak smile touched her lips.

Jennifer kissed her cheek. "Mom, I was so afraid for you."

She straightened and saw her mother's gaze move around the room. A look of alarm came over her face.

She bit her lip. "You're in the hospital, Mom. Paul has been admitted too. He's hurt, but he's alive." She stroked her face. "Please don't worry."

Rick squeezed her hand. She looked at him, a question in her gaze.

"I was down to see him before I came back up here," he said softly. "He's conscious and asking about your mom."

She said a silent prayer of thanksgiving. "Did you hear that, Mom? Paul is conscious too."

Tears welled in her mother's eyes and spilled down her cheeks.

She brushed them away. "It's all right, Mom. I know you probably feel lousy, but the doctors say you'll be all right in a few weeks."

"How long?" her mother asked, her voice low and raspy.

"That you've been in here? You were bought in on Saturday. Today is Monday...early evening."

"How is...Paul?"

"He's hurt pretty badly, but we've made sure he wasn't alone."

"We?"

"Me, Rick, Cherica, and Jayson. We've all spent most of the last three days taking turns sitting with you both."

"Rick? Your Rick?"

"Yes." She turned and exchanged a quick smile with Rick. "Yes...my Rick. This is my mom, Rick. Mom, this is Rick Markham. I called him after I got here and he and his friend Troy came and sat with me. Yesterday, Cherica got back in town and she's been here on and off since then. She had to work today, but she stopped by for a lightning visit this afternoon. Jayson will be here when he gets back in town in a few days."

She saw her mother's gaze lock with Rick's. "So you're Rick. She loves you," she said.

"I love her," he said after a noticeable pause.

"Are you sure?"

The pause this time was less noticeable, but still long enough to trouble Jennifer. "Yes."

"You'd better treat her right. I won't always be in this bed and if you don't, you'll have to answer to me," she warned.

"I've learned my lesson, Mrs. Rose. I won't risk losing her again or... incurring your wrath."

She nodded and closed her eyes.

Jennifer frowned, released Rick's hand and touched her arm. "Mom? Are you all right?"

"Yes, darling, but I am tired. How long did you say you'd been here?"

"On and off since Saturday morning, mostly on."

"Then I want you to pay a quick visit to Paul and then take your Rick and go home and make love."

Jennifer blushed. "Mom!"

"I'm sure you're wound up. I'll be fine. You just go home and make love." She opened her eyes and looked Rick. "You have a lot to atone for."

"I know that."

"Mom, he has nothing to atone for," she protested. "He didn't do anything. I'm the one who has to make atonement."

"No." He turned her to face him. "You have nothing to atone for either. I shouldn't have been so bullheaded."

She smiled. "Oh, I don't know. I'm rather fond of blond, bullheaded men."

"Take him home and make love to him," her mother said.

An hour later, Jennifer and Rick sat together on her sofa, close, but not touching.

Although aware that he wanted to make love, she knew they needed to talk first. "I'm so sorry for not believing in you, Rick."

"Why didn't you? That's what I couldn't understand. Once we started seeing each other regularly, I never looked at another woman." He moved closer and clasped one of her hands in his. "I couldn't understand how you could really think I wanted another woman. I want you, Jennifer and only you."

She took a deep breath. "I guess I just found it so difficult to believe that a man as handsome as you could really love me."

"Why should that have been so hard to believe? You are one of the most beautiful women I've ever met. You're sweet, funny, passionate, and you like sports. Why shouldn't I have fallen for you?"

"A lot of men are turned off by my being a full-figured woman."

"That's their loss," he whispered brushing his lips against her neck. "You are a warm, beautiful woman with an exquisite, sexy body. I adore you."

She leaned against him and he put an arm around her. She pressed her cheek against his shoulder. "I've always loved men with blond hair," she said. "When I was in college, I fell for three of them. I thought they loved me, but all three of them ended up hurting me. I was just a novelty to them."

She bit her lip. "The last one even told me I couldn't really expect him to get serious about a girl he couldn't pick up without straining every muscle in his body."

"Oh, Jenn. Honey, he was obviously an idiot. You know I don't feel that way."

She nodded. "I know, but surely you can understand his point of view."

"No, I don't. I fell in love with you, just the way you are. I don't need or want you to lose weight, tone up, or do anything except love and want me as I do you."

She lifted her head and looked at him. For the first time, she saw the love and adoration she had never expected to see in his beautiful eyes. "I do both of those things already, Rick. I think I have since our first night together."

He stroked her cheeks and kissed her slowly. "Me too."

"But, Rick, are you sure?"

He cupped her breasts in his hands, rolling her nipples between his fingers. "I'm positive. Look, you probably wish my hair wasn't blond."

"That's not true," she denied, running her fingers through his hair.

"Yes it is," he insisted. "But it's all right. I can deal with that. Neither one of us expected to fall in love, but isn't that what makes what we feel for each other so incredible? Because it was so unexpected."

She was silent for a moment. A smile touched her lips. Because the unexpected nature of their attraction helped provide the extra spark that had characterized their relationship almost from the moment they met. "And so doubly appreciated," she added, lifting her lips for his kiss.

He kissed her slowly, several times, while he fondled her breasts and stroked his hands over her stomach. Her heart thumped and she felt a rushing dampness between her legs. Lord, she needed to feel his cock in her again.

"Your stomach is not big enough," he whispered, unbuttoning her blouse.

She laughed. "You're nuts. It's way too big. It always has been."

He lifted his head and stared into her eyes. "You're not pregnant."

"No."

"Then it's not nearly big enough." He stood up and urged her to her feet. "Let's see what we can do to change that."

She put her hands against his chest. "Rick, I love you so much and I want to have a baby, but not before I'm married."

He sighed, arching a brow. "Okay, you want to play hardball?" He pushed her blouse off her shoulders and unhooked her bra. "Okay, if you ask me nicely, I might be persuaded to accept your proposal."

She shivered as he tossed her bra aside, exposing her breasts. Her skirt followed. Kneeling, he leaned back to look at her in her thong underwear. "Damn, Jenn, you are one beautiful woman." He stroked his hands down her body. "I love your body." He pressed warm kisses along the inside of her legs that made her knees buckle and her pussy drip.

"Oh, Rick! Rick!"

He leaned forward and pressed several kisses against her thong-covered mound. He then slipped his hands under her thong and slowly peeled it off. He rained kisses along her legs as he did.

Moments later, she stood in front of him naked and deliciously aroused.

He leaned forward and buried his face against her mound. She felt his tongue parting her pussy and dipping inside. A ball of heat tightened her stomach. She moaned softly.

"God, I love the way your aroused pussy tastes and smells," he whispered. "I love the smell of you wanting my cock in you." Gripping her hips, he settled against her and began eating her. He alternated between kissing her cunt and lapping at her clit. When he inserted first one finger, and then another inside her, her legs threatened to collapse. She trembled and gushed against his mouth.

He lapped at her juices, gave her pussy and clit one last kiss, and transferred his attention to her butt. Kneeling behind her, he began covering her cheeks with warm, languid kisses. "God, I love your big, jiggly ass. Did you know you have the cutest ass dimples?" He licked her cheeks and gently parted them.

She thought she was in heaven when he inserted his finger up her and fucked her slowly. She'd never dreamed having anything in her ass could feel so damned good. Her pussy began to cream all over again. "Oh, Rick. That feels so good."

"Glad you like it, honey." He gave her ass a final kiss and a deep thrust before rising and facing her.

She leaned her forward against his shoulder. "Hmm." She glanced down and saw his cock straining against his pants. She pressed her hand against the bulge between his legs. "Hmm. This feels nice."

"Nice is too tame a word," he murmured, his voice husky.

She smiled. "I think you said something about wanting to marry me," she teased.

He scrambled out of his clothes and took her in his arms. "If you ask me nicely and fuck me once or twice, I might be persuaded."

His nude body felt so good against hers. It had been so long since they'd made love and they'd never made love secure in the knowledge of their mutual love. "Oh, I plan to fuck you all right," she promised, linking her arms around his neck. "But first I need you to know that there hasn't been anyone else since we stopped seeing each other."

"I have to admit that I've been horny as hell since, but I haven't been with any other woman since the first time we made love."

She fondled his cock and balls. "And what have you been doing to alleviate your blue balls?"

"God gifted me with two hands that both work rather well." He lifted her chin and brushed his mouth against hers. "Of course I'd rather have been inside your sweet pussy, but they worked in a pinch."

"Oh, my poor, darling. Let me give you a taste of the real thing," she said.

In her bedroom, she straddled his body and slowly impaled herself on his hard, bare cock. They both moaned and thoroughly enjoyed their coupling. When he was fully seated in her, she reached back and fondled his balls.

"Oh, damn, Jenn." He gripped her hips and shoved his cock up into her pussy. "Fuck me. Fuck me, Jenn. Fuck me hard and fast. Fuck my cock, baby."

"Ooh, Rick. I think I was born to fuck you. You complete me and make me so happy. I love you so much."

He rubbed his thumb against her clit. "Prove it. I need a little less talking and a lot more fucking."

A tingle of pleasure radiated out from her cunt and down to her toes. Bracing herself with her arms, she lowered her body and quickly began to fuck her pussy down onto his thrusting cock. He wrapped his arms around her, widened his legs and pushed roughly into her. She moaned and clung to him, her whole body awash with pleasure. Knowing he loved her made what was happening between them so much sweeter. They fucked and thrust wildly at each other until her toes curled, her stomach muscles tightened and clenched, and her pussy exploded.

He came moments after her, spewing his seed directly into her still quivering channel. She moaned and pressed her face against his shoulder. "Oh, God! Oh, lord, Rick! Oh, that was so good."

He curled his fingers in her hair. "I love you so much," he whispered.

"Are you sure?"

"Positive. I know I should have told you before, but it's not so easy for me to say."

"Me either, but I do love you."

"In that case, will you marry me?"

"I'll think about it," she told him sleepily, feeling warm, safe, and very secure in his love.

He laughed and bit into her shoulder. "You either marry me immediately or risk getting fucked senseless until you do," he warned. "So what will it be? Are you going to marry me or do I have to get physical?"

She licked his shoulder. "I've always wanted to be fucked senseless by a big, handsome blond," she laughed, then trembled in anticipation when he rolled them over so that he was now lay on top of her, with his cock still buried deep inside her.

"All right, you asked for it." He lifted his weight onto his arms and began thrusting into her.

She closed her eyes and surrendered her heart, soul, and body to the man she was so madly in love with.

Much later, they lay in her darkened bedroom, cuddling and talking. "Rick, why didn't you fuck my ass the day I came to your office? I know you wanted to."

"I did want to. I still do, honey. But I was hurt, angry and near losing control that day. If I had fucked your ass, I would really have hurt you physically. And I wasn't so angry I didn't know I didn't want that." He kissed her. "Besides, I knew you were afraid."

"I was, but how did you know?"

"I just knew. Besides, it was bad enough that I took your pussy without giving you any consideration or pleasure. There was no way I was going to rip into your ass and hurt you like that."

"You made up for it when you made love to me on the sofa."

"No I didn't. I know I hurt you emotionally and physically that day and I am so sorry, honey."

"You didn't hurt me anymore than I must have hurt you, Rick. I can't believe I was so silly. Let's just chalk that day up to a learning experience and try to ensure it never happens again."

He kissed her. "You are such a forgiving sweetheart."

"I love you. I have also from day one."

"I love you too."

"From day one?"

"I have no idea when it happened. I just woke up one morning and knew I was really in love for the first time in my life."

"The first time? Really?"

"Like this…yes. Oh, there have been other times when I thought I might be in love, but… it was nothing compared to what I feel for you, honey."

She smiled. "Rick, what would have happened if I hadn't called you out of desperation?"

"Desperation?"

"I only called you because I couldn't reach Cherica, Jayson, or Julie."

His hand on her breast stilled. "Jayson? Who is Jayson?"

She heard the sudden sharpness in his voice and smiled slightly. "He's the friend I was with when we met at the club when you were with your blonde supermodel," she teased, gently nipping the nipple closest to her.

"Oh...him."

"Yes...him. You'll like him when you meet him."

"Maybe," he said cautiously.

Her smile widened. "You will. He has no interest in me beyond our friendship. He's rather sweet on Cherica."

"He is?"

"Yes."

"She's a pretty woman. They'll make a good-looking couple. Is she sweet on him?"

She sighed. "Yes, but she has...issues that keep them apart."

"What issues?"

She shook her head. "They're not my issues to discuss. We've digressed enough. Now answer my question. What would have happened if I hadn't called you?"

"I was going to call you. I'd finally realized what a fool I'd been for not trying to see how that stupid kiss must have looked from your point of view. When I think of the grief that skinny bitch caused us, I could almost wring her neck."

She felt the tension in him and stroked her hand down his chest and lower. She never tired of touching his flat, hard abs. "Oh, don't be so hard on her. Who could blame her for wanting to kiss you?"

He sighed. "Anyway, I thought I'd start my comeback attempt by sending you red roses. That's what I was about to do when your mother called me. Why did she call me, by the way?"

She brushed her lips against his chest. "I begged her not to but she was determined to make you see reason," she said. "And don't ask me how she got your phone number and full name because I haven't got a clue."

"That much I know. Paul told me he found out for her."

"He did?"

"Yes. It seems one of his friends is a private detective."

"Oh."

"Now for a really important question. When will you marry me?"

"As soon as my mother gets out of the hospital." She stroked her hand down his stomach and over his cock and balls. She never tired of touching him, even when his cock was flaccid.

"Big wedding?"

She shook her head. "No."

"Why not? I thought all women dreamed of a big, formal white wedding."

"Is that what you want?"

"Of course not, but I will happily participate if it's what you want."

"It sounds tempting," she admitted. "But that type of wedding take a long of time and preparation and I think we should get married as soon as possible."

"Why?"

She gave his cock a gentle squeeze and smiled when he groaned in protest. "Because I want to be your wife before I have your baby."

"Babies," he corrected. "As in at least two. Can do?"

"Yes. Oh, yes, Rick."

"Good. Of course if you keep squeezing my dick like this you'll sterilize me," he said, peeling her fingers from his cock.

She laughed and settled against his shoulder. "Sorry, but I love holding and squeezing your dick. It's so big, thick, and hard — everything a dick should be."

He laughed. "I'm glad you approve."

"Oh, I more than approve...I'm enchanted...and in love."

"Yeah? With me or my dick?"

"Both of you, but I'd still love you even if your dick wasn't so big and hard." She stretched out a hand. She sighed with satisfaction as her fingers closed around his cock again. It slowly began to thicken again. "But I'm glad it is."

He brushed his thumb against her clit before gently inserted two fingers into her pussy. "I think someone wants some more cock," he teased.

She hesitated. "Rick...awhile ago you said you still wanted to fuck me up the ass."

"I do."

She swallowed. "Well...you have a hard cock and I have a willing ass." She closed her eyes and rolled onto her stomach. "So lube up and fill my ass with cock. Just...go slowly."

He lay on her and she bit her lip. His cock up her rear would probably hurt like hell, but she would grit her teeth and bear it because he wanted it.

He kissed the back of her neck, stroking her thighs. "You are one big, sexy woman, and I love and adore every damn ounce of you." He urged her legs apart and rubbed the head of his shaft along her outer lips.

"You do?"

"I do for a fact, my beautiful, darling. I love all your lumps and bumps. I wouldn't change a single damn thing about you and I couldn't bear to part with even half an ounce for love or money. You totally enchant me and I love you madly, my lovely, lovely Jennifer."

She was so hot and excited she trembled helplessly under him. "Oh, Rick! You mean that."

"Damn straight I do, my lovely Jennifer."

"In that case, you are definitely going to be allowed to fuck the shit out of my ass."

He licked her neck. "Delicious, raunchy invite my beauty, but tonight I intend to make love to you...your pussy."

She felt a sting of disappointment. "Don't you want my ass?"

"More than you know, but I need too much sex from you tonight not to hurt you if I got up your delectable ass. We'll save your ass for our honeymoon. Deal?"

"Yes, just put your cock somewhere in me!" she pleaded.

He laughed and sank his cock inside her and they made love. They took their time, kissing and caressing and fondling and touching each other, as if they were making love for the first time. The feelings flowing through her were magical and wondrous. She loved him and loved how making love with him felt. When they came within seconds of each other, Jennifer decided that was a sign that they were going to be happy together.

"I love you," she whispered.

He brushed his lips against her neck and curled his body against her back. "I love you too and long before we have our first baby, I'll make sure you'll never doubt that again," he promised.

There was an undeniable ring of sincerity in his voice. It touched a hidden spot of solid ice deep in her heart, thawing it. A warm glow infused her body and filled her with hope.

"I won't, Rick. My Rick."

"Yes. Your Rick, my lovely Jennifer. Always."

"Always," she echoed.

Rick woke in the middle of the night and nuzzled her breasts until she opened her eyes. "Hey you, what are you doing?" she asked sleepily.

He reached over and turned the lights on dim. "Are you sure?"

She blinked up at him. "Am I sure about what?" she asked, confused.

"That you love me and want to marry me? You...you're sure about that...right? I mean you haven't changed your mind...have you?"

She laughed, saw that he was serious, and sat up. She linked an arm around his neck and stroked her fingers through his hair. "Rick, darling, have you lost your mind? You know what a pushover I am for big, handsome, well-hung blonds. Not only do I love you madly, but I am hopelessly in love *with* you. I love you and cannot wait to marry you and have your babies. Is that clear?"

He nodded and pressed his forehead against hers. "Oh, damn. I can't believe you really want me."

"Can't, huh?" She stroked her hands over his shoulders. "Guess I'll have to make a believer out of you." She reclined on her back and smiled up at him. "Come get fucked, darling."

She sighed with pleasure as he pressed his big body against hers. His cock was already semi-hard. She pushed at his shoulders. He rolled onto his back. She positioned herself between his legs and cuddled his shaft in one hand. Sighing softly, she began to suck the big head of his cock.

"Oh, damn, Jenn. That feels so good...oh, damn...take a little more into your mouth."

Taking a deep breath, she sucked in more of his cock. It felt warm and thick moving over her tongue. She closed her eyes and savored the new sensations as she felt him harden and swell in her mouth.

"That's it, honey. That's it. Now touch my balls," he whispered, cupping a big hand over the back of her head. "Suck a little harder, baby."

Breathing in the sweet heat emanating from him, she sucked greedily at his cock.

"Squeeze my balls gently," he moaned, shoving his hips forward.

More of his dick slid over her tongue and down into her throat. The muscles in her stomach clenched and her pussy creamed as realized he was about to ejaculate down her throat.

She sucked harder and curled her fingers against his thighs as his release neared. To her relief, he withdrew his cock so that only the head of him remained in her mouth as he came.

She overcame her instinctive urge to gag and jerk away. She swallowed the warm, creamy seed until he sagged back against the bed. Then she lay with her face pressed against his groin. He reached out and urged her up to lie beside him. He pressed his body against hers and kissed her. "Damn, I love you."

"I love you too," she whispered, burying her face against his damp shoulder.

"I know you do."

"And I won't ever mistrust you again."

"Well, you'd better not. Because if you do, you'll have to suck my cock all night long to atone for your sins," he warned.

"Suck your cock all night long, huh?" She stroked her hand over his stomach, brushing the tips of her fingers over his flaccid dick. "I have news for you, buddy, I like the idea of sucking your cock. It was a real turn on when I felt it swelling in my mouth and you coming against my tongue. That's what I call a vanilla milkshake."

He laughed and hugged her against him. "Oh, damn, woman I love and adore you."

She grinned. "Are you bragging or complaining?"

"Stating a fact. I am hopelessly in love with you."

She laughed, feeling carefree and completely happy. "Yeah? Well, join the club. I fell for you the moment I saw you."

"Oh, you talk too much," he complained, slipping a finger into her pussy. "What say we work on getting you pregnant?"

"Yes, please," she said meekly, rolled on to her back, and parted her legs in open invitation.

As he rose above her, she closed her eyes, and knew the weeks, months, and years ahead would be everything she had ever dared hoped they'd be. She was in love with and loved by a man who fulfilled her every want and need. How could the future be anything but wildly wonderful?

Once his cock slid deep into her pussy, she gave up her efforts to think and concentrated on feeling all the bliss and joy attached to making love and loving the big blond she adored. And who, thank God, adored her right back. Every fat ounce of her. Yesss!!

About the author:

Critically acclaimed Marilyn Lee is an Ellora's Cave best-selling author. In addition to writing erotic romances, she also enjoys spending time with her large extended family and rooting for all her hometown sports teams. Marilyn's other interests include collecting pulp novels and Marvel comics. Her favorite TV viewing consists of forensic shows, westerns, and mysteries. She's also seen nearly every vampire movie or television show ever made. (Forever Knight and Count Yorga, Vampire are favorites!)

She thoroughly enjoys hearing from her readers. You can write to her c/o Ellora's Cave Publishing at P.O. Box 787, Hudson, Ohio 44236-0787 or email her at Mlee2057@AOL.com.

Coming Soon:

Three reigning queens of erotic romance. Three titillating tales of lust and love set in future worlds. One highly anticipated book…

VENUS IS BURNING

ISBN # 0-9724377-5-4

A futuristic erotic romance anthology

Devilish Dot by Jaid Black
Hot To The Touch by Marly Chance
Road To Rapture by Marilyn Lee

COMING SOON:

PLEASURE QUEST

A futuristic erotic romance anthology

Marilyn Lee
Mary Winter
Christine Warren

Printed in the United States
22866LVS00001B/70-726